Homemade Love

Also by J. California Cooper

A Piece of Mine
Some Soul to Keep
Family
The Matter Is Life
In Search of Satisfaction
Some Love, Some Pain, Sometime
The Wake of the Wind

Homemade Love

J. California Cooper

St. Martin's Griffin New York

 For information, address St. Martin's Press, 175 Fifth Avenue, New York, N.Y. 10010.

Library of Congress Cataloging-in-Publication Data
Cooper, J. California.
Homemade love.
I. Title.
PS3553.05874H66 1986 813'.54 86-3970
ISBN 0-312-19465-x

10 9 8 7 6

DEDICATED WITH LOVE
TO

Joseph C. and Maxine "Mimi" Cooper, my parents
Paris Williams, my chile
Shirley May, a sister I lost

others

Robert & Versi   Lovey & Watt   Lanisha Cherie   Mabel
Lorenzo Tucker   Undeen Thompson   Rodney Cooper

and

All those people, through all the years of this world, of all races, with love and kindness in their hearts and a conscience in their minds who have helped people of their own and all other races suffering travail, the pain of life, pressed upon them by those without love, without kindness or a conscience.

Contents

Acknowledgments

Especially Alice Walker for thinking my work good enough to publish my first collection of short stories as her first publication with her partner, and now my friend, Robert Allen, at Wild Trees Press. What would I have done without them!

Paris Williams, my daughter, who is 100 percent behind me in everything I dream of doing.

Shy, for listening. Joseph, for encouragement.

Mary Monroe, author, for her helpful heart.

Joyce Carol Thomas, author, for all her helpful information on my writing journey.

My editor, Michael Denneny, for his knowledge, responsiveness, and, always, consideration of me. His excellent work will never be forgotten.

My co-editor Paul Liepa, who always kept his word and gave me every assistance available to him.

Every Reader who has liked my work. Thank you so much.

Author's Note

I choose the name "Homemade Love" because it is love that is not bought, not wrapped in fancy packaging with glib lines that often lie. Is not full of false preservatives that may kill us in one way or another. Is usually done from the bottom up, with care, forethought, planning, and consideration for others. It is work done for the reward, that is the reward. Is usually solid, better and memorable. Is sought after. Do not think only of food either. Many more things, the best things, were all made at home, first. The Stradivarius, the first beds, even toilet paper.

Homemade goes a long way. Usually lasts longer than we do.

So, I said, I would like some Homemade Love.

Have some.

HOMEMADE LOVE

Swimming to the Top of the Rain

Mothers are something ain't they? They mostly the one person you can count on! All your life . . . if they live. Most mothers be your friend and love you no matter what you do! I bet mine was that way. You ain't never known nobody didn't have one, so they must be something!

Life is really something too, cause you can stand stark raving still and life will still happen to you. It's gonna spill over and touch you no matter where you are! Always full of lessons. Everywhere! All you got to do is look around you if you got sense enough to see! I hear people say they so bored with life. Ain't nothing but a fool that ain't got nothing to do in this here world. My Aunt Ellen, who I'm going to tell you about, always said, "Life is like tryin to swim to the top of the rain sometime!"

One of the things I always put in my prayers is "Lord, please don't let me be no big fool in this life!" Cause you got to be thinking, and think hard, to make it to any kinda peace and happiness. And it seem like things start happening from the moment you are born!

My mama died from my being born the minute I was born! Now if you don't think that changed my whole life, you need to pray not to be a fool! She left three of us. My two sisters, I call them Oldest and Middle, and me. She had done been working hard to support herself for years, I learned, and finally for her two children after my daddy left. He came back, one more time, to make one more baby. I can look back now and understand, she was grieved and lonely and tired from holding up against hard times all by herself and wished this time he was back to stay and help, so she let him back in her bed. Probly to be held one more time by someone sides a child. Then I was made and she told him. He got drunk, again, but didn't beat her. There's some whippings people give you tho, without laying a hand on you, hurts just as bad, even worse sometime. He left, again. He musta broke somethin inside her besides her spirit and her heart cause when I took my first breath, she took her last breath. I wished I could of fixed it whilst I was inside her, so she could live . . . and I could get to have my own mama.

She had already told my sisters what my name was to be. I was called "Care." My first sister was "Angel" and the second "Better," four and five years old. But I call them Older and Middle.

We was alone, three babies.

Mama had two sisters we had never heard of. Somebody knew how to reach them cause one, Aunt Bell, who lived in a big city, came and got us and took us in. Had to, I guess. Cause wasn't nowhere else we could go at that time . . . three of us!? Musta been a shock for somebody wasn't expecting anything like that!

We think my Aunt Bell was a prostitute. Older say she was never in the little rooms she rented for us but once or twice a month. She would pay the rent, stock up the food, give us some little shiny toy or dress, lotsa warnings bout strangers, and leave us with a hug and kiss. If she had a husband we never met him. We were young and didn't understand a lot, but we loved that woman, least I did. Was somethin kin to me in her. She was so sad, even when she was smiling and laughing. I didn't see it, but I felt it. I'd cry for her when I thought of her and not know why I was crying! She took care us for about five years, then she was dumped on our front porch, stabbed to death! We opened the door for sunlight and found her and darkness. That darkness moved right on into the house, into our lives, again.

I don't know if they even tried to find out who did it. Just another whore gone, I guess. Never mind the kind of person she was, trying to do for us and all. We had never really been full too steady, but we had always had something!

We was alone, again.

I found out early in life you going to find a lotta mean people everyplace, but sometime a few good ones somewhere. Someone came in and prepared for the tiny, short funeral. The church donated the coffin and fed us. Somebody went through Aunt Bell's few sad things she had there and that's when we found out we had another aunt, Aunt Ellen. People should tell the children where to look and who to look for, just in case! Do we ever know what's goin to happen to us in this life? Or when?

Somehow they reached Aunt Ellen and she got there bout a week after the funeral. We was all separated and could tell people was getting tired of feeding and caring for us. Well, after all, they was poor people or they never would have known us anyway and they was already having a hard time before we needed them!

Aunt Ellen was a husky-looking, mannish-looking woman who wore pants, a straw hat and a red flowered blouse. I will always remember that. I was crying when she came . . . scared. I stared at her . . . our new mama . . . wondering what was she going to be like. What would she do with us, to us, for us? Would she want us? I was only five years old and already had to worry bout my survival . . . our lives! I'm telling you, look at your mama, if she be living, and be thankful to God!

She picked me up and held me close to her breast, under her chin and she felt just like I knew my mama did. She took us all, sat us down and just like we was grown, talked to us. "I ain't got no home big enough for all us. Ain't got much money, done saved a little only. But I got a little piece of land I been plannin to build on someday and this must be the day! Now, I ain't got chick or child, but now I got you . . . all of you. Ain't gonna be no separation nomore, you got me. I loved my sister and I love you."

Three little hearts just musta exploded with love and peace. I know mine did! I remember holding onto her pants, case she disappeared, I could disappear with her!

She went on talking as she squeezed a cheek, smoothed a hair, brushed a dress, wiped a nose. "I ain't no cookie-bakin woman! But you learn to bake the cookies and I'll provide the stove and the dough!" My sister, Older, could already cook most everything, but we'd never had no stuff to cook cookies with. "Now!" she went on as she stroked me, "You want to go with me?" One nodded yes, one said "yes." I just peed I was so happy! I kept putting her as my mama! "We'll try to swim to the top of the rain together!" She smiled and I sensed that sadness again, but it went away quick and I forgot it.

When I hear people say "Homeland," I always know what they mean. There is *no place* like a home. She took us to that beautiful land on a bus, eating cold biscuits, bacon and pieces of chicken, even some cornbread. All fixed by our old neighbors. We stayed hither and yon while she mixed and poured the concrete and built that little cabin with four rooms. We lived in each room as it was finished. It was a beautiful little lopsided house . . . ours! Oh, other people came to help sometime, but we worked hardest on our own home! It took two more years to finally get a inside toilet and bath, but Aunt Ellen had to have one cause she blived in baths and teeth washing and things like that, tho I never saw her take one!

We lived there til we was grown. We tilled a little land, raised our own few pigs and chickens, and split one cow with another family for the milk. She raised us, or helped us raise ourselves.

Older sister quit the little schoolhouse when she was bout fifteen years old in the eighth or ninth grade and got married to a real light man. She just had to have that real light man! In a couple years she had two children, both girls. The light man left, or she left him and came home. Aunt Ellen said, "NO, no! I ain't holdin up no leaning poles! If you old enough to spread them knees and make babies, you old enough to take care yourself! You done stepped out into the rain, now you learn to swim!" Older cried a little cause I guess she was scared of the world, but Aunt Ellen took her round to find a job and a place to live. We baby-sat for her til she was steady. One day we looked up and she was on her own! And smiling! Not cause she was doing so good, but because she was taking care herself and her children and didn't have to answer to nobody! When her man came back, she musta remembered Mama, cause she didn't let him in to make no more babies!

Middle sister went on to the ninth grade, then went to nursing school. Just the kind teach you how to clean up round a patient. Aunt Ellen was proud. She was getting older, but not old yet, and said she would help anybody wanted to go to school long as they got a job and helped themselves too, and she did. That left only me home with her, but I didn't want to go nowhere away from her!

We didn't have no lot of money, helping Middle go to school and taking care of ourselves. I couldn't even think of getting clothes and all those kind of things! I had me one good dress and a good pair of patent-leather shoes I wore to church every Sunday. So after I got out the ninth grade I asked a lady who sewed for a livin to teach me in exchange for housework and she did. That's why I know there's some nice white people who will help you. After I learned, she would pay me a little to do little things like collars, seams and things. Then I still watched her and learned more for free! I sewed for Aunt Ellen and me and Older's babies. We saved money that way. That's the same way I learned to play the piano . . . sewing for the piano teacher. I got to be pretty good. Got paid a little to play at weddings. Cause I won't charge for no funerals. Death already cost too much!

Middle graduated from that school, well, got out. Cause all they did was ask her was she all paid up and when she said yes, they handed her a paper said she was completed. She got married right soon after that to somebody working in a hospital and they moved to a city that had more hospitals to work in. Soon she had a baby girl. Another girl was good, but where was all our boy children? They necessary too!

One evening after a good dinner, me and Aunt Ellen sat out on the porch. I was swinging and she was rockin as she whittled some wood makin a stool for her leg what had started giving her trouble. She wanted something to prop it up on. Mosquitoes and firebugs was buzzing round us. She turned to me and said, "You know, I'm glad you all came along to my life. I did a lot of things I might never have got to, and now I'm glad they done! I got a family and a home too! I blive we gonna make that swim to the top of the rain! Things seem to be workin out alright! You all are fine girls and I'm proud of you. You gon be alright!"

Pleased, I laughed. "Aunty, you can't swim goin straight up! You can't swim the rain! You got to swim the river or the lake!"

She smiled. "Life is more like the rain. The river and the lake lay down for you. All you got to do is learn how to swim fore you go where they are and jump in. But life don't do that. You always gets the test fore you learn the swimming lesson, unexpected, like rain. You don't go to the rain, the rain comes to you. Anywhere, anytime. You got to prepare for it! . . . protect yourself! And if it keeps coming down on you, you got to learn to swim to the top through the dark clouds, where the sun is shining on that silver lining."

She wasn't laughing, so I didn't either. I just thought about what she said til I went to sleep. I still ain't never forgot it.

The next day when dinner was ready, Aunt Ellen hadn't

come in from the fields and it got to be dark. Finally the mule came home dragging the plow. I went out to look for her, crying as I walked over the plowed rows, screaming her name out, cause I was scared I had lost my Aunt Mama. I had.

I found her under a tree, like she was sleeping. Had a biscuit with a little ham in it, still in her hand. But she wasn't sleeping, she was dead. I couldn't carry her in and wouldn't leave her alone so just stayed out there holding her all night long. A kind neighbor found us the next day, cause he noticed the mule draggin the plow and nobody home.

I sewed Aunt Ellen's shroud to be buried in. I played the piano at her funeral too. Her favorite song, "My Buddy." I would have done anything for her. I loved her, my Aunt Mama, She taught me so much. All I knew to make my life with.

I was alone again.

Older and I buried her. Middle ~~couldn't~~ didn't come, but sent $10.00. I gave the preacher $5.00 and stuck the other $5.00 in Aunt Ellen's pocket, thinking, All your money passed out to us. . . . Take this with you. Later, I planted turnips and mustard greens all round her homemade grave, cause she liked them best. Then . . . that part of my life was over.

I was alone again, oh Lord. Trying to see through the rain. You ever been alone? Ain't had nobody? Didn't know what to do? Where to turn? I didn't. I was alone even with my sisters living. This was my life and what was I to do with it?

The house and land belonged to all of us. I tried to stay in that cabin, intended to, but it was too lonely out there. Specially when all the men started passing there late at night, stopping, setting. Rain coming to me just like Aunt Ellen said. I didn't want to be rained on, so I gave it out to a couple without a home and moved on down there where my middle sister was, in the city. I got a job living-in and was making a little extra and saving by doing sewing. I was hunting out a future.

I went to church a lot. I stick close to God cause when you need a friend, you need one you can count on! Not the preacher . . . but God! I steered clear of them men who try to get a working woman and live off her itty-bitty money. I ain't got to tell you about them! They dress and sit while she work! No! No! My aunt taught me how not to be scared without a man til the right one comes, and that's why I'll have something for him when he gets here!

I met that nice man, a very hard-working man at a church social. Was me and a real light woman liking him and I thought sure he would take to her, but he took to me. I waited for a long time, til after we were married to ask him why, case he might think of something I didn't want him to think of. He told me, "I like her, I think she a fine woman, a good woman. But you can't like somebody just cause they light! Ain't no white man done me no favor by making no black woman a baby! What I care most bout skin is that it fits! Don't sag . . . or shrink when it gets wet!" He say, "I love your outsides and your insides, cause you a kind and lovin woman who needs a lotta love and don't mind lettin me know it! I need love too!" Then I knew I could love him with ease. And I did, through the years that passed.

My husband was a railroad-working man so we was pretty soon able to buy us a little home and I was able to stay in it and not go out to work. I made a little extra money with my sewing and teaching piano lessons. We was doing alright! We both wanted children but didn't seem to start up none, so I naturally came to take up more time with my nieces. That's when I came to know the meaning of the big importance of who raises you and who you raising!

I had urged Older to come to the city with her two girls, they were bout fourteen and fifteen years old round then. Middle didn't have no husband now, and her daughter was bout thirteen years old. I could see, tho they was all from one family, they had such different ways of doing things! With my husband gone two or three days a week, I had time to get to know them more.

Now, Older,.she the one with the two daughters, she did everything for the oldest pretty, light one, leaving the other one out a lot. The oldest one had more and better clothes and was a kinda snotty girl. Demanding . . . always demanding! She was going to be a doctor, she said, and true enough she studied hard. She volunteered at the hospitals a lot. Getting ready, she said. She was picky bout her clothes and since her mama didn't make too much money and wouldn't let her work, she was always asking me to sew for her or do her hair. Her best friend was a white girl, live up the street, from a nice family.

I took to sewing, buying the material myself, for the youngest brownskin one. She was a little hard of hearing and didn't speak as prettily and clearly as her older sister, so they was always putting her off or back, or leaving her home when they go out. Now, she was not college-smart, but she was commonsense smart and a good decent girl, treated people right. That's what I like, so I helped her! She was never asking for nothing but was grateful for the smallest thing you did for her. That kind of person makes me remember my aunts and I will work my butt off for people like that! I was closest to her.

I spent time with Middle too. I love my family. Her daughter, thirteen or fourteen years old, was a nice quiet girl. At least I thought she was quiet. I found out later she was beaten under. She was scared to be herself. Her mother, Middle, had turned down her natural spirit! You know, some of them things people try to break in their children are things they may need when they get out in that world when Mama and Papa ain't there! The child was tryin to please her mama and was losing herself! And she wasn't bad to begin with! Now, it's good for a child to mind its mama, but then the mama got to be careful what she tells that child to do! She's messing with her child's life!

Middle was mad one day and told me she had whipped the child for walkin home holding hands with a boy! I told Middle, "Ain't nothing wrong with holding hands! Specially when you heading home where your mama is! Humans will be human! Some people wish their fourteen-year-old daughter was only holding hands!" I told her, "You was almost married when you was her age!" Middle told me I didn't have no kids so I didn't understand! I went home thinking children wasn't nothing but little people living in the same life we was, learning the same things we had to. You just got to understand bout life! I hear people say, "I ain't never been a mother before, how am I supposed to know what to do?" Well, let me tell you, that child ain't never been here before, been a child their age before either! How they always supposed to know what to do, less you teach em! How much do you know to teach em?

Several months later she whipped that girl, hard and long, for kissing a boy in the hallway. I told Middle, "She was in your hallway. What could she do out there and you in here?! If they was plannin anything special, they got the whole world out there to hide in!" Middle said, "I wish she was just out there holdin hands walkin home, stead of this stuff!" I looked at her trying to understand why she didn't understand when she was well off. "While you think you whipping something *out* of her, you may be whippin' something *in*! Talk to her more. Are you all friends? You know, everybody need a friend!"

She was so sad, my sister, I asked her, "Why don't you think about gettin married again? Get you some kissin stuff? Then maybe natural things won't look so dirty to you! You can be a mama and a wife, stead of a warden!" Middle just screwed up her face and say she know what she doing! Sadness all gone . . . madness too close. Things you feel sposed to make you think bout em! Think how you can help yourself. Hers didn't. She say, "The last thing I need is a man messing up my life again!" Well, it was her business, but it looked to me like she was gettin close to the last thing! I told my niece if she ever need a friend, come to me. I was her aunt and her friend, just like Aunt Ellen was to me! I left.

Life is something, chile! Sometime watching over other folks' life can make you more tired than just taking care your own!

Older's snotty oldest daughter had graduated with good grades from high school and was going out to find work to help send herself to college. Both she and her white girlfriend planned to go to college, but the white friend's family had planned ahead and had insurance for education. They both went out together to find work. They went to that hospital where Oldest's daughter had volunteered steady, spending all kinds of time and energy in most all the departments there. Her friend hadn't. But when they had their interviews, her friend got the job! Well, my niece was just done in or out, either one or both! But her white friend told her, "I'm a minority, aren't I? I'm a female! At least one of us got it! That's better than some man getting it!" Ms. Snotty just looked at her and I don't think they're friends anymore, least not so close. Anyway, my niece wrote a pack of letters and a month or so later, she went on East and got a job. I can tell you now, she didn't become no doctor, but she is a head nurse of a whole hospital. Her mama surenuff scrimped and saved and made herself and her other daughter go without to keep that girl in school. I was giving my other niece all she had to keep her from feeling too neglected. I loved that girl! I loved them both, but people with certain kinda needs just get me!

Middle had told her daughter, "No company til you are eighteen years old and through with school!" But she didn't give her the hugs and kisses and touches we all need. So the girl found her own. She was sixteen years old now, and she had gotten pregnant. She and the boy wanted to get married but Middle beat her and demanded on her to get an abortion. The girl wouldn't have one, so Middle was going to show her how her evil ways had cost her her mother, and how lost she would be without her! She put her child out of her rented house! Her own child! Seem like that was the time for Middle to act like the mother she was always demanding respect for! That was going to be her own grandchild! But . . . she put her out. I didn't know it and that poor child didn't come to me. . . . What had I missed doing or saying to show her I was her friend? Oh Lord, I prayed for her safety. You know on the other side of your door sits the whole world. The good people are mostly home taking care of their family and business. It's the liars, thieves, rapers, murderers, pimps, sadistics, dopers, crazy people who are out there . . . waiting . . . just for someone without no experience. Thems who that child was out there with, the minute her mama slammed that front door! And a belly full of baby, no man and no mama. It's some things you don't have to live to understand. I wanted my grandniece. I would have taken care of it for her. And Middle would love her grandchile. It's a mighty dumb fool won't let their own heart be happy! If she was worrying bout feeding it . . . she got fed! And didn't have no mama! Trying to show what a fool her daughter was, she showed what a fool she was! Your chile is your heart, your flesh, your blood! And sometimes, your way! Anyway, life goes on. I couldn't find her til way later.

Older's daughter had done graduated and was a surgical or surgeon nurse, and had her own place and car and everything! Older was planning to go visit her and did, leaving the youngest daughter to stay home and watch the house with my help. When Older got back she was hurt and mad. She didn't want to tell it, but we finally got it out of her. Her snotty daughter had made her wear a maid's uniform, the one she had for her regular jobs. She had to cook and answer the door and stay out the way when company came! Not tell nobody that was her daughter! Can you believe . . . even can you imagine that?! Her mother!? Well, it's true, she did and she still does it! Then, shame of all shames possible to snotty sister, her young sister got a job as a maid in a whorehouse! Snotty and Middle hated that, but she made such good money, tips and all, and the girls giving her jewels and discarded furs and clothes and all. They wanted to use them, borrow her money but seem to hate her. Two ways. For having these things and for being low enough to work as a maid in a whorehouse! They made her sad. She was trying to swim to the top of the rain in her own way. I tried to love her enough, but there ain't nothin like your own mama's love!

Bout that time somebody told us about Middle's daughter. She was a prostitute trying to pay her own way, raising her daughter, living alone. She didn't have time to find a job before she started starving, so this was a way. She was trying to swim to the top of the rain, but was drowning. Middle took a gun down on that street and threatened to kill her! I talked to the young woman. She was still a good girl, just lost! But, loving her baby! That baby had everything! Was the fattest, cutest, sweetest, smiling baby I ever seen! Ohhh, how I wanted that baby! And I knew the pain, the great big pain I could see in her face she was going through. Who *wants* to sell their body? The *only* thing, no matter how long you live, that is truly yours, is your body. I don't care how much money you got!

Later, Middle told me, "Ohhhhh, I wish she was home just having one of them illegal babies! Oh, just to have her back home holding hands, or kissing in the hallway, even having that baby! I shoulda let her marry that boy when they wanted to! I'd rather kill her than see her be a prostitute!" She hurt and I could see it. It was the first time she had even blamed herself a little bit for her part in all this. I had a little hope for her.

The daughter brought the baby her mother had tried to make her get rid of and let her keep it sometime. Middle loved that grandchile so much, cause you see, she didn't have nothin else in her life. It was empty! I kept it whenever I could. That girl, her daughter, stayed sad . . . sad . . . sadder. She would look around her mama's house and make a deep sigh and go away looking hopeless. Her mama told her to come home, but she said it was too late.

I got involved round that time with Older's youngest daughter. She had fallen in love and was bout to marry a blind man. I thought that was good after I met him. He was so good-seeming, so kind to her, so sweet and gentle with her. My sister was going crazy cause he was blind! She didn't even think of his honesty and kindness and love for her daughter. She could only see he was blind. Oh Lord, deliver the innocent from some fools that be mothers, fathers and sisters. She married him anyway, bless her heart, and my sister had a heart attack . . . a real one! Her daughter she didn't love so much and her blind husband took care of her, better than she took care herself when she could. Her nurse daughter, said she couldn't! Didn't have time.

I was so busy being in my family's business I hadn't been in my own enough! My husband, have mercy, told me he was leavin me cause he had met someone he might could love and she was pregnant! I looked at him for bout a hour, it seemed, cause he was my life but I hadn't been actin like it! Been giving everybody else all my thoughts, time and life. But I had done learned bout happiness and I understood if he wasn't happy here, he should be where he was happy! Ain't that what we all live for? How could I get mad at a man who had give me everything, including the chance to make him happy? I washed, cleaned, packed his clothes, and let him go, clean away. Then I went in the house, took the biggest bottle of liquor I could find, sat down and drank for bout a week. Now, I ain't crazy and a hangover ain't the best feeling in the world. Life started again in me and bless my soul, even alone, I was still alive!

I went out in my . . . *my* yard and saw one lone red flower, dug it up and took it in the house. I told it, "You and me, we alone. We can survive! I'm going to plant you and make you grow. I'm going to plant me and make me grow. I'm going to swim to the top of this rain!" I planted it, it wilted, it lay down even. I let it alone cept for care. Let it grieve for its natural place. I loved it, I talked to it. I went and put it back outside, it's *my* yard too! It could be mine and still be free where it wanted to be! In a day or two, it took hold again . . . it's still livin! Me, I just kept carrying on with my swim.

I hadn't seen nobody, cause I didn't want to be bothered with their problems, I had my own! Then Middle came to me. My niece was in the hospital, dying from a overdose of dope in her veins! Ohh Lord!

When I got to the hospital, I stood in the door and listened to my sister talk to her daughter who could not hear her. "Don't die, my little girl, *don't* die! Stay with me. You all I got. What I'm gonna do . . . if you die? Stay with me, don't leave me alone. Hold hands with anybody you wants to! I won't say nothing! Kiss anybody you want to . . . I won't mind at all. Just don't leave me, my baby! Have many babies as you want! I'll love em all! Don't go. Child of mine, you can even be a prostitute. I don't care! Just live. I rather see you on dope than see you dead! Cause if you got life, you got a chance to change. Baby, I'm sorry. I'm *sorry*! Be anything you want . . . JUST LIVE . . . don't die! Come home! *Don't die*!" She screamed that out and I went in to help her grieve . . . cause the beautiful young woman was dead.

After the funeral, the good thing Middle had left was the baby she had tried to make her daughter get rid of. Her daughter had won that battle at the cost of her life, it seemed . . . so now, Middle was blessed to have someone to love and be with . . . in her empty life. I went on home to my empty life.

Things smoothed down. God is good. They always smooth down if you give life time.

One day, bout a year later, my doorbell rang and when I answered it, my husband was standing there with a baby in his arms who reached out for me the minute I opened the door. I reached back! I ain't no fool! He had got that young woman he thought he loved and she had got him, but after the baby was born, my husband wanted to rest and stay home when she wanted to play and go out. She left him with his baby. I tried to look sad for him, but my heart said, *"Good, Good, Good!"*

But he didn't look too sad. We talked and talked and talked and talked! I loved my husband and I knew he loved me, even better now. He wanted to come home and I wanted him home. And I wanted that baby. It was his and I musta not been able and she was. How lucky I felt that if I couldn't have one, he had give me one anyway. We didn't need to get married, we still was. Neither one of us had gone to the courts, thinkin the other one would. So I had a family.

Sometimes I hold my baby boy and look deep in his little bright, full of life eyes. I know something is coming in the coming years cause life ain't easy to live all the time. Even rich folks commit suicide. But I tell my boy, like my aunt told me, "Just come on, grow up, we gonna make it, little man, right through the storms! We gonna take our chances . . . and get on out there and take our turn . . . swimming to the top of the rain!"

Living

I was born in the country. Stayed there all my life cause I didn't never see nothin wrong with it! Didn't never look up over them hills and wish I was monst all them bright lights and them crazy people what dwells in them cities! I musta been satisfied and was too big a fool to know it, as it turned out. I found out it's some truth to them sayings I have heard all my life and let em just slip through my head without really thinking bout what they meant! Or I just got too old to remember what they meant! I started thinking bout this was a big world and what I might be missing. Well, let me tell you! The grass ain't greener nowhere! You ain't missed nothin if you been satisfied! One of them sayings sure is right! Ain't no fool like a old fool!

Now, I use to get up of a morning and look around my little house. It's a small little thing, but, facts about it, it was the best I could do! I keep it whitewashed and my wife keeps it clean as a pin. She a O.K. wife! After I look over my house I go out in the yard, look that over too. Look at all the green things growing. Fresh vegetables for food and my stomach. Pretty little flowers for my soul, so my wife say. I look at my strong friend, Babe the dog, and my wife's little cat, Honey.

Didn't have to work no more cause I had started early, could quit early! So I guess I didn't have no real big worries. For a long time, I'm over fifty years old. Just being outside, on my little land, feeling the wind on my face, summer breezes, autumn breezes, winter winds, and the spring sunlight, was all good enough for me!

I don't know what went wrong, but one morning I woke up and all them things had changed seemlike. The house looked old and beat out! My wife, who used to be mighty pretty, was old and beat out, looked ugly to me!

I'd go outside and all them growing things didn't look like nothin but work! Seen them weeds I done pulled yesterday just come right back up and stick they tongue out at me! The dog was laying around like he had worked fifty years and the cat sat around scratching fleas! Facts about it, things just wasn't right no more! I just couldn't get right! With nothing!

Now, I am still mighty good-looking and it seem to be all going to nothing! Just wasting away like old age is a disease! I looked myself over real good and well . . . facts about it, I really did look alright! Better than alright! But for how long!? That's the time I decided I was going to do something with myself and live a little! I had done paid my dues for it!

One night I poured me and my wife, Dotty, a glass of berry wine we had made and told her, "Listen here! I think I better go way for a while!"

Dotty looked at me like I was crazy! "Go way? Where? Where you going?!"

"Well," I said, very serious cause I meant business, "let's face facts! You ain't enough for me no more! This house ain't enough and this town ain't enough! So, there it is." Then I realized that was it in a nutshell!

Dotty looked at me like I was the nut in the shell for a long time so I drank my wine down and poured me another one. Showing her I was grown and could do whatever I want to!

"Why?" she finally said.

"Because," I answered as truthfully as I know how.

"Because why?" she asked again. I always did have to explain everything to her twice!

"Because . . . because I ain't happy nomore!"

"Have I done something wrong to you?" she whispered.

"Something . . . facts about it, everything wrong to me. I can't put my finger on it tho!" I took another drink.

That woman threw her sewing down and hollered, "Are you crazy!? My hand shook, only for a second tho, as I poured another drink and told her, "No! I ain't crazy! I'm tired! And I'm . . . I'm . . . I don't know how to splain it to you, but facts about it, I am! And I am going to leave here . . . for a while. You can wait for me do you want to! If you don't . . . well, that's up to you. I don't care no more! But you need to try to do somethin bout yourself fore you try to go anywhere cause, Dotty, girl, you done let yourself go! You ain't pretty nomore! Facts about it, you is pretty doggone ugly!"

Now, I know I shouldn't have said that. Dotty has been the best wife a man could have! I ain't never even thought of another woman all our married life. Well, maybe I thought of one or two, but not enough to do nothin with em! Dotty was all I needed. I don't know what was wrong with me but I wanted to hurt her! But mostly, I just didn't care bout nothin!

I packed a ole cardboard suitcase we had round here, then decided I wasn't goin to no fine city with a raggedy suitcase like that, so I packed a shopping bag with some underwear and my suit and a roll of toilet paper, and while she stood at the door with her hands on her hips and crying at the same time cause she don't understand me, cause I'm a man!, I left. Caught me a bus cause I blive it's faster than anything else cept flyin and I didn't feel like, ain't never felt like, flyin! Went on up bout fifty miles to the closest city round here.

Lawd, lawd, lawd! That city is a mighty thing! Everything moving! Everything bright and busy! Facts about it, the city is alive! Alive! Tall buildings and wide streets. Sidewalks big as a whole road where I came from! Lake right in the middle if the bus station is in the middle, cause it was cross the street! Trains on tracks stopping every block to pick up and let off people who walk and run, going somewhere! People who laugh and talk and pat each other's back and tip hats! Women with long pretty legs, all colors! Some dressed nice, some better, some not so good. But they all moving . . . going somewhere!

I liked it! This where I belong! I thought I better find a room first and unpack and wash up, then get on out and see more of this great big *pret-ty ci-ty*. I made my way over to the part of town I could afford. Don't know what area it was, just know it's over by a hospital. The Welcome Angel Hospital.

I got a little ole dinky room with no view outside. Had a few roaches and I could see leavings of a mouse. Had a steady little drip in the basin, but that's where I put my little snacks I had from the bus station, cause I know how to beat a roach and a mouse cause they don't like water! Somebody had left a ole sweater on a nail in the closet and I took my piece of toilet paper and covered my fingers while I picked it up and dropped it by the door, gonna give it to the landlady later so she could know I knew she had not done cleaned that room up. But what the hell! I thought I'd get a better one later. It shouldn't cost no more than this one. I know she thought I was a country hick and was cheating me! But, facts about it, I knew in a few days I'd know my way round this city and would be waving her a backhanded goodbye!

I washed up . . . with cold water! Hot water spigit wouldn't turn. Then I hit the streets!! I blive that's how they say it!

First thing, right off, I see a place named Dusty Dig Inn—Happy Hour. Well! That's what I came here for, so I went in . . . Happy! I sat down and ordered a whiskey, then changed to a beer cause the prices was too high, not happy at all! I was sitting there looking around, smiling at everybody when it got so I could see in the dark. Then this lady came over. Well, when she said, "Buy me a drink, darling?" I ain't no square! I know what she was cause I done read about them and seen them on TV. All that makeup and tight skirts and all. Her hair was mingled dirty and her fingernails too. But what's the hell! I bought her a beer. Hell! It's my first day in the ci-ty!

Now, I'ma tell you something! And I ain't shamed of it . . . really! I ain't slept with but two women in my life! One before I got married and the one I married. For almost thirty years I ain't had but one woman . . . my wife. So I said, "Facts about it, Seymor, that's my name, it's time for you to sip from the glass of life! It's your turn!" So when she talked me into it, I let her and was taking her home, well, to my room. Just as we was leavin, a fight broke out between some men playing cards at a back table. One had a knife and he was starting to slash! I told her, "Let's get out of here!" She said, "No, let's see what's happnin!" I told her, "I don't want to see nobody kill nobody, I'm going!" So she came too and we went to the room. We did what we came for.

I didn't like it cept for a second or two, cause she kept all her clothes on and made me keep mine on too! Shoes and all! Hell! I was paying $5.00! Least let me take my shoes off! But she didn't, and when it was over she left. As I look back now, I'm glad that's all it costed and she didn't have one of them rough fellows bust in on us! Anyway, I washed up and went on back out cause now I was hungry.

I was just turning a corner, going in a different direction so I could see another part of town, when I saw someone I use to school with and I hollered his name, "Henry! Henry!" He must didn't hear me cause he turned into a house and I ran after him. When I got to the house, the door was left open, but I rang the bell anyway. I got manners! Well, when there was no answer, I pushed the door open and hollered again, "Henry!" He came round a corner, but he was backing up and a man was pushin on him and a crazy woman was there screaming! From what I could tell before I blacked out, the man was waving a gun saying he was going to shoot Henry bout his wife! Seemed he had done stayed home from the swing-shift job he had just to catch him! I heard a shot, then I fell backwards down the steps!

When I got out of the Welcome Hospital later that day, I

wasn't too messed up. Just a bandage or two. The policemen asked me questions, but they could tell I didn't have nothin to do with that stuff!

I was surenuff hungry now! So I went to find a place to eat. Every place was crowded . . . and expensive! I finally went in one I could afford and finally got a table. It was for two people so the waitress asked did I mind somebody sharing it. I said no. She went and brought somebody over and left. They said, "Listen, I am gay . . . so if you have a problem with that, I'll get another table cause I don't want no mess while I eat!" I say, "Heck no! I'm glad to meet somebody that's happy for a change! I'm happy myself!" I got a funny look but he sat down. We had each ordered our own when these two burly-looking men came up and asked him to leave and start pushing on him! Well, facts about it, they beat him up! Then turned to me and said, "Are you gay too?" real mean! The last thing I remember saying, before everything went black is, "I was!"

Well, I was welcomed back to the Welcome Hospital and when I came out, I had a few more bandages. One round my head now. But I was starving! They may welcome you but they don't feed you in that hospital! You just lay round and wait, and wait and wait!

It was dark when I went home, well, back to that room, and washed up best I could. I was limping a little now, too. I wanted to go to bed but I was hungry and the landlady said she didn't have nothin to give nobody! Specially nobody been getting into trouble all day! I went back out to eat.

I found a spot not too far, bout four blocks, and went in quietly. I told the waitress I want to eat *alone*! Facts about it, I don't like no trouble! Ain't never had none before! I saw another man in there with a cane hanging on his chair and wondered did he just get into town too.

I ordered the juicy beefsteak and mashed potatoes and gravy, glass of buttermilk, and was gonna get some dessert later. I sat back waiting and feeling better as the time went by cause it was low lights and all and the music was low. People talked softly. Food cost more here but I was looking for a better class of people! The waitress brought my food and I was getting ready to cut and eat, when the table right cross from me, a woman in a nice wine-colored suit and big hat called the man with her a mother______ (you know) and put her cigarette out in his face! He hollered and reached for her and she grabbed a glass and broke it cross his head! I tole her, and I was almost cryin, I said, "Oh miss, Oh miss, you don't want to do that! You a lady!" She turned to me with eyes that was all red and brown and mad, with the devil standing right there in the pupil. She turned to me, her lips curled back, and she said, "Mother______ (you know), I'll wrap this table round your head!" And was getting up!!

Lawd, lawd! I got up and flew, a bottle hit me back of my head as I grabbed that cane hanging on that man's chair, 'cause it was hurting to run! I left wishing I had grabbed my steak in my hands.

They welcomed me again at the hospital for my head was cut a bit. When I came out, I went home, well, to that room. The rats and roaches had ate my little cakes and things from the bus station. Just waded right on through that water! So, I went on to bed. I felt like crying, but when I cried it hurt, so I couldn't.

The next morning, *early*, cause I want to miss some of these crazy people if I can, I went out to eat. But, facts about it, the streets was still full! Can you blive that! These people ain't got sense enough to go home!

I limped on down the street, but least I had a cane. I'd mail it back to the owner, but don't know his address. I found a place that nobody was in. Good lawd! I went in fast as I could. The cook was alone, so I ordered a great big breakfast and ate it all! Eggs, sausage, pancakes, hashbrowns, two cups coffee, glass of juice, and two glasses of milk. It hurt to chew, but I was hungry! I paid and left, smiling.

I hit the sidewalk, smiling, and this man with a picket sign ran up to me and hit me in my stomach, as hard as he could! I didn't hear but half of it, but I think he said, "You dirty scab!"

When I came out the hospital, all my breakfast was gone. All my mouth didn't throw up, my behind threw out! They did leave me my cane tho. Thank the Lord for that! I was thinking He had done forgot me!

I stood still outside that hospital a long time. Scared to go anywhere and scared to get too far away if I did go somewhere. There was a park cross the street and I could see kids playing. I love children and know wherever they are, there is some peace. I limped on over there and sat on a bench mongst the kids. I guess I sat there ten or fifteen minutes when a little girl came to sit beside me, then a little boy. We talked and I thought of my children and when they was growing up. I was reaching in my pocket to give them a nickle or a dime, when something hit the back of my head, on both sides! Then whipped me with my cane.

Somehow, the police believed me and I could understand them women, but, why . . . why do people want to stay where you can't hardly be friends with nobody? *Plus* this time the doctor said I had some clappin or somethin and I had to take some shots!

When I came out the hospital this time I still had my cane back. I went straight to that room and I didn't even wash up, just lay down. I had to stay another day, for another shot. Lord, how I hurt! I layed up in that dirty room and thought and thought and thought. Lord have mercy on all people who call this living! Have mercy on me too! It was cold in that room and I ended up putting that dirty sweater on over my suit!

When the doctor let me go, I went to that room and packed my shopping bag and headed for the bus station. *Going home*! Home! Thank God I got one!

I was sore all over and facts about it, I knew I wasn't handsome nomore! I had done aged a hundred years in two days!

City life is hard on you! The bus driver wouldn't let me on the bus. Said he couldn't take no responsibility with a man as bandaged as I was. I had to go allll the way over to the train station. Had to walk cause my money was bout gone and I didn't know what the train cost. I finally made it. My mind kept tellin me, "Tomorrow, tomorrow, tomorrow!" cause I knew I would wake up in my own sweet, clean, quiet bed, side my own sweet, clean, beautiful, wonderful wife! You hear me!!?

I got on the train and started for a seat and the conductor said, "Where you goin?" I said, "Up there to sit down." He said, "No you ain't! You going back there," pointing. I said, "Cause I'm black?" He said, "No! Cause you broke! I can see that without looking hard. Get!" I got! I looked out the window by my seat, looking at the world and thanked God for every mile flying by taking me to my dear wife and my beautiful little house with the sweet, quiet garden and the peace and the love and the food and the bed.

When I hobbled up to my house, my wife was at the door watching me make my way. She came out and ran to me, her arms stretched out and I was yearning, trying to hurry to get to em! When I got inside the gate, that little picket gate I had built and put there, I made her help me get down on my knee, only one was useful, and let me kiss *my* ground!

Facts about it, I ain't had another boring, sad, tired day at home again. And when my son comes from the city to visit us, I don't fuss . . . cause I know he's tired! I say, "Come on in, son, and rest!! Cause I know you tired!"

Happiness Does Not Come in Colors

My mama always said I was the busiest, talkinest child she ever did see! But it's so much to talk about! It's a big, big world at the same time it's a small one. And it's so much goin on! I'm very smart too, so sometime I notice things like . . . love seem to make everything the same. Just like sometime hate makes everything the same. It just all depend on what you feel that makes up what you see.

I don't really have no right to talk cause I ain't really never been nowhere and done nothing. I got to be thirty years old and hadn't even been married and had no children.

It wasn't all my fault tho, cause where I live is a small town up here bout seventy-five miles from New York. But who needs a city if New York is so close?! New York got everything so we didn't need everything here. It's a few black families here, but everybody mostly stays to themselves til something like a wedding or a funeral comes up. Once or twice a year maybe we have a dance and everybody comes, even some of the white folks.

Now I want to make it clear that I like some white folks. Some of them are really nice, human people. Not greedy and full of hate. The rest of em I can't stand! Cause of history and some other things happening today that will be history next week!

It's mostly farming done around here, livestock and things. I don't like that kind of work! Something I must have inherited from some old great-grandmother was a slave or something! I blive that stuff comes down to younguns. And I'm mighty careful to stay away from things even look like they close to slavery.

I remember during them times when they was having freedom marches and sit-ins and stand-ins, ever what all they was, we was tryin to get *in*! I saw it on TV and my mama and daddy read it in the papers. Me and my best friend, she's a Indian, use to sit on her porch eatin some of that good bread her mama baked and talk about how we wish we could go somewhere and march. Her mama talked Indian language so I asked her, "How come your mama don't talk American?" She told me, "She *does* talk American! We're speaking the first American language!"

I told her, "Maybe if you spoke that white man's talk you woulda known better when one of em was lyin to you!" She was my best friend but she didn't like to talk about that, so we went back to talkin bout marches and freedom! That was the day her mama went to the store to get some beans and when old Mr. White who owns the store gave her less than the two pounds she paid for, she asked him to weigh them again. He wouldn't! He told her to leave em or go! Well, they got mad at him but couldn't decide what to do, how to fight it. Who was they going to tell that it happened all the time? The white sheriff who leaned on Mr. White's counter drinking pop spiked with liquor? No! So I decided to watch him.

One day my mama gave me 50¢ for two pounds of beans. Mr. White weighed em so fast, snatchin em off the scale, that I asked him to weigh them again. He said, "You kids get outta here!" He started to put the beans back so I said, "My mama wants them beans! Give me my beans!" He growled, "Pay for em and get on out!" So I did. But I walked to the small department store, went to the scale department and weighed em. They weighed one and three-quarter pound, bout! I told my mama and she went to the store. Mr. White told her I musta spilled some cause his weights was right, then he showed her, gave her a new bag and said don't send me in there no more!

My chest was poked way out in front bout my mama! And she pat me on my back for lookin out for her money. I thought about it while I went to sleep that night and the next day I got my best friend and we made up two signs. One said, SOMETHING AIN'T RIGHT—I THINK IT'S MR. WHITE! The other one said, MR. WHITE CHEATS! Then we went back and marched in front of Mr. White's store!

First, and soon, Mr. White ran us away. We went back. Then the sheriff ran us away. She had to go home, my friend, but I went across the street and marched. When they ran me away from there, I went up to the corner and marched, carrying both signs! Then the sheriff went and got my mama, brought her down here and she got me. When we got home I waited to see was she going to whip me for standin up for my rights. She said, "Have a piece of cake and a glass of milk and rest." I smiled and loved her. Then she said the best of all. "I bet Mr. White will think twice before he cheats anybody again!" Well, that's what I wanted to hear—that I had made something right! Even the white ladies that shopped there started checking the scales! But that got old and there wasn't that much cheatin you could find round here, so time passed and I grew up a little more while I was waitin for something to come along.

I was so happy when this black lady named Joyce moved here and rented that veterinary man's house. He had moved to the top floor of his office after his wife died, leavin his house empty for a long time. Joyce rented it and I went over to meet her and ended up with a little job of helpin her settle in. It wasn't real bad, just dusty and spider webs, mice, and a few snakes trying to keep warm.

I was glad cause jobs and friends are hard to find in a little place like this. We got two groceries, two gas stations, the post office, one little department store, one bar that's always full, one hamburger shop with hot dogs, and, see, that's all! Mostly family-owned. If you need a job you got to go in business or leave town, one or the other!

Joyce came in like the wind. She kept me busy. I ain't never seen a Black woman with all her gumption! And all that stuff she had! Books, piano, records, thinkin games, fishin stuff. Oh, she had plenty more things! And running round the country all by herself! She is something! Bout in her forties and a real nice-looking woman wearing that natural hair, real soft and pretty and neat. She was not skinny and not fat, just in the middle. Now, what I liked best, she had all kinds of books and pamphlets and things talkin bout freedom and fight for your rights! Black power, Black economy, and stuff like that. She said she had gone all over the country fightin for equal rights for all! Not communist, just tired of not being treated right by white folks who she say run everything in sight and some out of sight too! Her husband had got killed in some march and she was right beside him! Ain't no sense in tryin to say by who. They never did catch em. But if he was black and fightin for his rights, we know who killed him! They even kill other white folks who are tryin to fight for equal rights for everybody. She was alone now and from what all she say, she planned to stay that way. I told her she came to the right place to stay that way cause I'm bout thirty and ain't never been no way but single! Sides, it's mostly white men here and she couldn't stand white people no kinda way, she said.

We use to sit and talk a lot.

She say, "I'm never going to find the kind of man I want nowhere, noway in this world! I don't even think of bein married. I'm tired. I need a rest. Besides, my last husband would be too hard to beat!! When my man died, the fire in my house went out!"

I say, "Well you safe here, honey."

She say, "I'd be safe anywhere."

So I say, "What kind of man would you want?"

And she say, "The kind I want ain't been born or he's already dead."

But since I want to know somethin about men, I keep on. "Yes, but if you did want one, what kind would he be?"

She thought a minute then said, "He'd have to be an honest man. That would take me a hundred years to find right there!" We laughed and she got up to pull down some curtains.

I said, "Okay, honest and what else?" I got up and started folding the old draperies, tryin to keep workin so she will keep talkin. I was trying to see what kind of man I should look for.

She smiled as she moved a piece of furniture, then got serious. "And kind. He would have to be kind. And clean. Like to laugh a lot. He's got to love animals. Like to go fishin. Love music. Like at-home games . . . and good food, even cook a little! And just so I don't never marry on a mistake, he has got to build me a home . . . all my own! Now, there! Oh, yes, and have a little money left over!"

I laughed. "Wow! You sure fixed it so he be hard to find!"

She puffed a pillow. "Above all, he has got to be Black!" She looked sad a minute. "Oh, I never will neet him. I'm sure he's somewhere I'm not. Or done been killed . . . dead."

Now, Mr. Brady the vet was white. All that spring and summer he was coming by to see how she was doing and all, with the house, of course. She use to get mad when she would see him coming up the drive. "He ain't doing nothing but tryin to see if this Black is tearing down his house. What he need to keep coming around here for? I pay my rent on time! Shit!"

But I didn't think he was coming round for that. Even tho I ain't been around much as she has, I know bout some things. He was always stopping in the living room where the piano was, looking through her records when she let him. Her music was always playing, you see. Sometimes Billie Holiday, Erroll Garner, or sometimes somebody named Motzart! Mr. Brady would talk about his flute he played. She would just stand with her arms folded looking at him and patting her foot softly. If he was in the kitchen, he would look at her seasoning shelf or something and talk about how he used certain spices in such 'n' such a thing. I know he wanted to look in them pots what was smelling so good with the steam coming up in the air. But he knew better cause she would say, "Vet man, don't you put your fingers on my pots! I'm the tenant, not the cook!" He would laugh a little lonely smile, wave his hand and walk slowly out the back door. She wouldn't let him use the front door even in his own house! Said, "I pay the rent til he take it back, its my front door! Somebody see that white man going out my front door might get the wrong idea!"

Flower, that's my Indian friend, liked Joyce too. She gave us so much good advice. About living and growing up being something and doing something with our lives. We thought we was too old. Bout to be thirty and all. She told Flower she ought to study law cause, she said, "That's what white folks mess with you with! They make the ones they need as they need them. Their friends pass them, specially if they against some other race and then they can do what they want to you. Cause you been made against the law!" She said Indians really need some lawyers so they could fight that shit! I ask her what I needed and she said, "Learn something that will make you independent. Like for going into business or something. Learn about money! They got classes for that! Save 10¢ out of every dollar you ever get for the rest of your life and learn what to do with it. Cause you gonna need some money! Forever!"

Out of some of her books she helped us find places for grants and also what schools and colleges to apply to. I looked up one day and Flower and I was going off to learn some knowledge. Flower left her daughter with her mama. Said they was all staring misery in the face anyway, so why not try for something better? We, me and Joyce, took her to the station. She had a purse full of addresses and things Joyce had given her and a suitcase full of all we could get together to add to her own. Then we were waving goodbye. I was lonely for her, but not for long cause my date was set to leave and I was going to stay closer to home by going to New York to junior college. Junior college but still a college!

In the meantime Joyce said she had to find a job or move back to New York. Well, I surely didn't want her to go! She had only been here bout two years and my life was changing for the better because of her. So one day I mentioned it to Mr. Vet what she had said. The next time I went by Joyce's house she said Mr. Vet, out the clear blue sky, had said he would like to set up some kennels for certain animals he needed to keep awhile, and some for people who left pets while they was on vacation, and if she would feed them in exchange for her rent and a few dollars he would get somebody else to clean em up. She told him she would clean them up with help, so they had a bargain! He started building them kennels right away. I could see he liked to be around that house that he had rushed away from before. And she stopped patting her foot when he came around. I never told her what I told him. She was happy again cause she was still independent. After a while she even stopped folding her arms when she talked to him!

When it was time for me to leave, I was so happy I was silly. I was only going to be gone about two years. Flower ended up staying away five years all together, coming home in between. I was all set up to stay in a nice rooming house with a friend of Joyce's and had a part-time job lined up except for the interview. I'm tellin you, Joyce was a good friend. There ain't many would take their time to help somebody. Sometime your own family won't do it! And here she was, a stranger! She was very careful bout her time too. Said all of it belonged to her at last! Still, she helped me and Flower change our lives.

I got the job, cause I meant to! I started college and it wasn't no snap! I'm thirty and had forgot how to study and think in this new way. So many new things were coming at me. Oh, I loved it! Pretty soon, in six months or so, I caught myself *thinking* even when I wasn't trying! Lord, Lord!

I was looking better, much better, cause I made my own money to buy things and I could sew, naturally. I was learning about money and its magic. How you can work magic with it, if you just understand it! I was saving not 10¢ but 25¢ out of most every dollar I made. Well, I had the grants too and my rent was low. Chile, I just didn't see no end to how far I could go!

I met a man about my age going to college also. He liked me, but I didn't even like his name . . . Jason, much less him. He was so square to me. Dressed so dumblike. I knew he was poor and trying to save his money for a better college. We took a lot of the same classes. I found he had a few dreams about what he wanted to do and I kinda started liking him. But I thought his squareness would rub off on me to the other students so I avoided him most of the time. That man would sometime walk about seven miles from where he lived to where I lived and I would hide and tell them to tell that old square I wasn't home. He even gave me a picture he spent some of his dear money for and I threw it in the back of a dresser drawer, slammed that drawer shut and forgot it. I also had forgotten all those years when I was just longing for somebody, anybody, to pay me some attention. I was Ms. Hot Stuff studying in college now, on a campus full of boys and men, who, I got to tell the truth, didn't hardly pay me no mind. Well, sometimes when they needed help with some homework!

I went home for Xmas vacation to show my mama and Joyce how good I was turning out. Flower had come home a week earlier and you know what that woman had done? She was new at this law stuff but she had done some learning cause the landlord was fixing up that house she and her mama rented! Another thing, the agency who was handling her mama's money? Found out they had been giving her less than she had coming, for years! That was on its way . . . soon! She ended up talking to Joyce about what to do with it. Joyce told her, "Buy some land with your own house on it. That will be some land nobody can take back when they see something they like on it." Flower did just that. Bought a piece of land with a house on it and bought her mama a new stove, refrigerator, washer and dryer. Her mama liked to sleep on the hard floor so Flower bought her a Japanese bed, king-size! Laws were changing their lives now that Flower was beginning to understand them. I was checking myself out with the newspaper, making penny investments, trying to see how good I was at it. Sometimes following Jason's advice, which was always good it seemed.

Jason didn't have anywhere to go for Xmas vacation. No family except a mother who was in a hospital somewhere and they never expected her to come home again . . . too poor . . . no home. I didn't want to be bothered with him so I left without telling him. After he walked that seven miles, they told him.

I went to see my friend Joyce, of course. Joyce, who was still hating white folks, was going fishing at least twice a week with Mr. Vet, who was still white. I mentioned it to Joyce that she was changing. She said with a grin, "He may be white, but he is fair and honest and that's all I need to know. They must not all be the same after all." She was packing a lunch at the time, for another fishing trip. He was too! They took off and stayed out there all day! Just them two! I said, "Well!" Soon I was heading back to college.

I decided to move nearer the campus to increase my chances of meeting more people and getting a husband to take me away from my little country town forever. I moved in with a girlfriend I had who was always surrounded by men. Very popular. We had a nice little place, fixed up nice and breezy. We had plenty company. I was having a natural ball! I didn't tell Jason where I was living.

I really was having a ball, only they drank a little too much for me and missed a lot of classes. A fellow that always came with the group started paying me attention. He never had before. I was thrilled. One day we all played music, dancing. He danced me right on in my room. I was laughing and being witty just like a fool. When I looked up I had been screwed and almost didn't realize it, he moved so fast! It was over and he was gone! Now, I'm going to tell you two things. One, I didn't plan on making sex with him. I'm after love and a husband. Two, everything that looks good, ain't! Don't have to turn out to be nothing! A lots of girls were after him and there wasn't really nothing to be after . . . if you know what I mean.

I felt pretty cheap for some reason, thinking, "Lord, how can I look that boy in the face after he been under my dress?! All in my business!!" But I didn't have to worry. He hardly waved at me. His eye was on somebody new for the next night! My ego hurt a quick minute, but see, I knew I wasn't missing nothing! Hear me if you can! That evening when I got to my room and was putting things away, Jason's picture fell faceup and I looked at him a little different. He had respected me, really liked me. I let his picture sit on the dresser faceup this time.

I studied a little harder, played around less, but still joined in sometime. I watched that liquor tho, cause I wasn't going to have everybody on the campus saying they passed through me!

One night my roommate asked me if I wanted to go see a gambling joint and a after-hour place. Of course I wanted to go! I had heard about them and I wanted to see everything! I knew I wasn't going to drink too much so if there was a raid I could get out without staggering into some wall. I dressed and I knew I looked good. We went with a group of fellows, of course, cause we were ladies!

Well, honey, it wasn't nothin but a den, a joint, a dump! But the people inside made it look pretty . . . in the dark! They were dressed to kill! These cooks and domestics were sharp, all mixed in with the hustlers, prostitutes and pimps.

Only big diamonds could tell you who the pimps were and not always then! Some had diamonds they only wore on Saturday night. Little pieces of furs and great long pieces of fur around thin and fat necks, sweating in the smoke and heat of all that talking, laughing. Music blasting out hitting the walls, running down ears and throats. Faces with eyes open big but still not big enough to see everything! They must have been reading lips cause you could hardly hear a word . . . til you went into the crap-shooting rooms. Just a little cussing now and then cause they were concentrating in there.

I watched awhile in the gambling room, looking at all the men with all that money! Thinking of what they could do on the stock exchange. I asked could I play 50¢ and they hardly looked up, just went on playing. I asked again and a very good-looking man, who was holding the dice, handed them to me and said, "I will even put up your 50¢!" I laughed, taking the dice . . . threw them out and got a six. Somebody said, "Six is the point!" I threw them again and got seven. Somebody scooped up the 50¢ like a whiz. Handsome, smiling at me, said, "Now, you know little girls should do little-girl things." I smiled back, but I was disappointed! I didn't know then, but I know now, those dice did me a favor, the biggest, by helping me lose. Lord, I've seen, now, some women gamble and lose everything they had, just like a fool, then stand around the table and beg, or run off and turn a quick trick or something, bring that money back . . . and lose that too!

Good-looking took my hand and held it a minute then dropped it like a hot rock when they handed him the dice. I wandered on away after a while. You know when you aren't drinking too much, people who do tends to look stupid to you. I was not enjoying myself. The excitement was gone. Then good-looking came out of the back room and caught my eye, came over and offered me a drink. I was so anxious not to run him away, I took one. To tell the truth, I ended up taking about eight! We talked and talked, just silly fun, but the more

I drank the more sense he made. You know what? When I woke up the next morning in my bed, he was laying right there beside me! I don't even know how we got home! My home!

I woke him up to ask him how and why. Chile, that man didn't pay me no mind, just went on along his business with me! I soon forgot my own question and couldn't feel nothing but glad he was there with me. Honey that man knew more about lovin then gambling! It's some things I thought I never would say cause I'm a lady, but he made me say em! It's some things I thought I never would do, but he made me do em! Not all of em tho!

Later, I asked him didn't he have to get up for work, cause I had a class and a job. He told me, "When I hang up my pajamas I have hung up my working clothes!" Show you how you can hear and not understand, cause I laughed. I have to admit, however he graduated, it was as summa cum lawdy, chile!

I didn't mean to see him again, but do you know how it is? He didn't call me and I didn't have no number for him so I went over to the gambling joint by myself. He was there. Seem like that's where he always was, when he wasn't performing his "job"! We ended up at my place, again, with me wondering why he never took me anywhere else with some of his money!

Soon he was taking me out once or twice a week. I was even cutting some classes to cook for him, wash his silk underwear, give him a massage, whatever he wanted! Now, college was very important to me and here I was . . . letting it drop behind, all for this man! Cause he made me feel good.

I am not a loose woman, contrary to what you might think. He was the second person since that handsome mess I stumbled into the time I got high. I guess I was a square. But the truth is I really liked this man, even thought I loved him.

Time passed and I was happy to see him whenever I could. He had told me he had other women, that he didn't love but who helped him, so he couldn't let them go for me until he had made it big and had enough money to go off with me and live happy ever after. I'm so smart, I believed him!

One evening he came over to take me to dinner. I was excited about it cause usually he just came over to go to bed, about three or four in the morning. I said to myself, "Huh! I'm getting to this man!" I even got a little smart with him about things I thought he ought to be doing til he slapped hell out of me! I didn't like that! My mama hadn't ever slapped me in my face! I wanted to tell him to get out! but was scared he really would so I just cried and fell out cross the bed. He lay down and made love to me better than ever, then told me as I lay in his arms, "Baby, I need some money, bad."

I really wanted to ask him bout them women of his, but one slap is enough. I asked instead, "Why? What for?"

He answered, "I got to take care my bisness and my women done worked and got together all they can and it ain't enough!" He smiled that beautiful smile directly on me. "If they was half the woman I know you are, I wouldn't have this problem!"

I said, "I am?!" And it wasn't no happy "I am?" either! He just went on talking and holding me. I wanted to move away from this conversation but decided I better stay and get it all. I knew what was coming! My mama had already warned me when I left for New York!

He was saying, "I want to leave them alone anyway. Don't want nobody but you!"

My throat was tight, I had to whisper, "Nobody but me?" All of a sudden I didn't feel like I was thirty years old. Didn't feel so grown-up.

He licked my cheek. "Nobody but you." He kissed me. "I wish we could . . . I want us to make our own money! Not depend on nobody but ourselves!"

I said to myself, "I do make my own money, cause you ain't never helped me!" Funny how he looked different, not so good, when I knew he was getting ready to ask me for my money. Or, Lord forbid, ask me to hustle for him!

He went on hugging and kissing, telling me he needed $2000 right away and he knew where I could get it (while he waited for it) and how I could be showing my love for him!

How I would never regret it. How we could be together . . . forever. (Forever seemed too long all of a sudden!)

I thought of those women of his who thought he was going to be with THEM forever . . . and had already been using up their bodies for him. Done sold the most precious thing they would *ever* have . . . for him. I knew if I was very rich and wanted him, he would leave and never look back at them or what they had given up for him! I said one thing, cause I am proud of being Black and trying to go to college to better myself. I asked, "Why you want me to do that? Can't you appreciate a Black woman trying to live decent?. . . Go to college? Better the race?"

He leaned back, looking into my eyes, laughing. "College is for squares! Ain't no money in college! We get the money them college people make! They are tricks! Who you think supports them women out there on them streets?! All them people who done been to college! That's who!"

I wanted to shut up but had to ask him, "Was Ms. Cadillac a prostitute? Ms. Ford? Ms. Lord and Ms. Taylor? Ms. M. L. King? Ms. Johnson? Ms. Tubman? Prostitutes don't make this world go round! They got to wait out there on that street til some square bring them some money." I wanted to duck but was in his arms, so just tightened up.

Laughter all gone, he said, "Don't talk that dumb college shit to me!" He said some more things but you already know what they were. He made love again and I let him cause I liked him and the feelings he gave me. I knew I had to let him go tho, so I wanted all I could get before he wasn't in my life anymore.

We got up, bathed, ate breakfast while he told me what to do, how to act. Even told me what to wear, where he would meet me and what to say. I listened and watched him, with dying love cause I knew he didn't love me . . . might not even like me! One thing I remember my mama teaching me, and even from my own good sense. "Don't nobody who love you want to see you, or even hear of you, being in nobody else's arms making love!" She also said, "If you ever find a old whore who's happy, you done found the needle in the hay!" And she said if I did turn out to be that way, I look just as good in my own Cadillac as anybody else! Don't nothing but a fool give such hard-earned money away! I was thinking all these things as I watched him leave. Huh! He wanted me to pay him, to let me kill myself!

I kissed him goodbye, watched him as he strutted away, smiling. Then I packed my clothes. Heading home!

I wrote a note to my roommate giving notice. Called the college with an emergency, made a few calls for a new place to live when I came back. Then I went home to my mama. This time I carried Jason's picture with me.

I enjoyed being home around people I knew loved me! I was soon heading over to Joyce's house. Mr. Vet was there and they were playing a duet. She was on the piano, he was on the flute and the records were playing to accompany them. I said, "Uh-huh!" Later when I asked her about him, being white and all that stuff, she said, "He is peaceful and he is kind. He is fair and these are things I like. Besides, he likes to go fishing, he likes animals, and he can cook. He is sweet and he says he loves me. He likes music and can play it. What can I say?"

I said, "But he is white!"

She said a little angrily, "I didn't plan on loving no white man! I used to wish he would stay away from here. But he didn't! I got to know him and . . . one thing led to another."

I said, "Love sure must be something if it makes you change your whole mind about life! You really use to hate them white folks!"

She looked at me a long time, thinking, before she answered, "I don't hate white skin. It's some Black people that have whiter skin than some white people! That's what's wrong with white people, some of them, they hate skin, black skin, red skin, yellow skin, no matter what's inside it! I just hate what most white people, white exploiters, have done to this earth and to so many people on it for thousands of years. I didn't really know any white men like Mr. Vet. But he is all the things I like in my man. So I am not going to be a fool!"

I smiled. "Plus, he ain't poor!"

She laughed. "Plus, he isn't poor!"

I laughed too. "You sure changed! All the way from Black to white!"

She pointed her finger at me. "Happiness does not come in colors! It comes from what's inside people, not what's outside! I wish sometimes. . ." She looked off into space. "I wish he might be Black . . . but I rather he be kind, honest, loving and loyal . . . in any color at all."

I laughed with her about other things, then I left to walk home. She had put something on my mind . . . Jason! Talking about kindness, loving and loyal!

When I got back to New York, I took Jason's picture out and bought a frame for it, putting it on top of my nightstand. I called him and we started going out again. I began to see different things about him. He was still square, but so was I, and I liked him that way now.

My mama had put $100 down on an old car with a $350 balance so I would come home more often. We split the payments. Jason kept it running. He knew how to do so many things! We went to see his mother too. She wasn't too sick, just old with no home to go to and couldn't get any money for herself til she had one. That worried Jason. He studied and worked hard trying to get to where he could do something for her. I liked her. She still laughed a lot and I found Jason did too, rusty unused laughter.

Of course I took Jason home to meet my mama. She really liked him cause of the way he was about his mama. He liked her and the small town too! He worked in the yard, trimmed the trees, and went fishing with Joyce and Vet.

Joyce was Mrs. Vet now and he was building her a house!

Over near the lake. She could almost fish out her windows now!

I told her, laughing, "That's what you said you wanted!"

She answered, not laughing, "Life's too short for lying!"

It was on that trip we made love for the first time. He hadn't rushed me. Don't nobody need to think a good square is a boring lover! I had heard that in school. It ain't true! He made love . . . with love. It don't get no better! We left there, exhausted and happy.

One day not too long after that trip, I was sitting in class and I thought, "What am I doing here? There are no stock exchanges in my little hometown! I sure don't want to stay in New York!" I called home, checked on a few things, then went to see Jason. We talked. Mostly about what we want out of life. Not to get rich. But a home, children, love, peace and happiness. All the things we need and some of the things we want. I told him my plan and he liked it. We included his mother. Oh, I loved him! Thank God nobody else got him while I was being foolish, growing up.

Now, I had heard from Flower. She was still in law college and doing a lot of things to help Indians all over America, but she was also getting married. He was a lawyer already. And he was white. I asked, "What you doing? I thought you were going to college to learn how to fight them!?"

She told me, "I found one who fights for me, with me! He loves me and my people. His family is so different. What can you do when you meet someone who is so kind and good? I love him." She was even moving her mama to her new home. That hit me.

You know, I had heard that old song when I was growing up, something bout, "The lovebug will get you if you don't watch out!" Them lovebugs are somethin!

Within two months, saving all we could, taking care of his mama's business, we all moved to my little hometown. We were married and moving into Flower's house cause it had more land and she was going to let us buy it someday when we could afford it. We did income taxes and paid rent for the whole year from that. Jason kept books for people and even drove out a ways getting new accounts we worked on together. The rest of the time we had for working in our garden, fishing . . . and making love. I really like that lovemaking, specially out here in the middle of nowhere, when it's raining and it's like nobody else in the world but us.

One day, looking up through the trees at the sky with my fishing pole between my legs, I thought about my closest friends being married to white men now and how happy they were. It was all so different from what it was in the beginning! There didn't seem to be any logic to this love stuff. Just happiness seemed to be what mattered the most. I thought about my happiness with Jason. Even with his mama who wanted a grandchild before she died. We did have enough happiness to share!

I turned to Jason who was casting for the hundredth time cause men don't know how to rest when they go fishin. I said, "Jason, let's start on us a family. Let's make us a baby fore you get too old."

Jason was trying to get his line untangled. If he had sat down and left it alone it wouldn't be tangled. He said, "Did you come out here to fish or . . ."

Then I remembered his logical mind, them accountants, you know! I said, "It's just logical. We got love, let's make a baby with it. Let's make twins. That's balanced!"

He threw that ole wooden pole out in the lake. Said, "Now . . . or when we get home?" Laughing.

I said as I fixed my pole in a tree, "Now! The logic of love is that you make it when you feel it!"

My logical little baby will be born some time next month in my little hometown, in our little warm house, to a mother and father who already love it. Two grandmas too. To happiness, I hope.

I'm going to try to teach it all I know to help it find its happiness someday. Cause it's hard to put your finger on just what it takes sometimes. But looking round me at my friends, I know one thing for sure. Happiness, love either, does not come in colors. . . . You may have different kinds . . . but the heart must not have eyes cause it ain't lookin at the color of nothing! The lovebug is blind!

Funny Valentines

Growing up in a big city makes you think you're in the middle of everything important! It wasn't until I went to the country with my family to get to know my daddy's people and my roots that I could see there was something else going on. In the city me and my friends all had the same idols and almost all the same ideas going round in our heads. We looked alike, dressed alike, talked alike, acted in what we thought was a hep way. Alike. In the country, people live farther apart and have to count on their own minds for entertainment. They have to do all their own thinking, use their imaginations, even just for toys and everyday play! Their talking even seemed more real!

I met so many relatives on that trip I thought everybody in the world must be my cousin. But the one I remember most of all is Dearie B.

I was ten and she was bout twenty-one years old when I first saw her. I'll never forget it cause it was Valentine's Day and Dearie B had made a picture of a heart and cut it into long pieces then pasted each piece on some paper and divided them among her family, giving her mama the biggest one. I asked why she didn't just make lots of valentine hearts then she could give everybody a whole heart!

She looked at me like I was crazy. "Cause I ain't got but one heart, silly! There's enough of that one for everybody to get a piece!" She made sense.

Now, in the city we would have called her "retarded," but in the country she was called "plain and simple" only. Just "simple" mostly. But what she said and did made sense so much of the time. You could tell tho, wasn't no great big brain growing in her head! She didn't read too well and when she got to a word she didn't know, she'd hit you with the book and stop tryin. She could count money very well tho.

Dearie B was tan-colored and had long pretty hair she loved to comb and braid. Fact is she liked to comb anybody's hair. She was always doing things. Wiping this, washing that! Clean as a pin! If she wasn't helping her mama, she was working in the garden or going over to her sister's to help her. She just helped everybody cook, sew, clean, whatever there was to do. She was such a regular-type person her mama had found a fellow for her to marry who was plain and simple like Dearie B but could run his family's farm very well. He had died tho and her mama hadn't found anyone else she wanted to trust with her own dear Dearie B!

Those days Dearie B was always taking flowers over to his grave and keeping that clean. That was her last chore in the evenings, then she would come home and just sit on the floor at her mama's feet while her mama combed her hair. Wasn't no beau in her life anymore, wasn't any marriage in her future anymore.

Sometimes she'd play with me like she was ten years old too. Sometimes she'd be a grown-up all a sudden and I'd get a whippin! But I always liked her, in between them whippin's.

After we left there, while I was growing up I'd get a piece of her heart on Valentine's Day with her message always scrawled like a child's, neat but large and unevenlike. I thought of her less but when I got that red strip of heart, I loved her again.

Over the years I finished growing up, got married, had babies, got divorced, married again. You know, just going on down the line! Dearie B was still at home with her mother, who was getting very old. My pieces of heart from her were getting larger and larger, cause first her daddy died, then a brother, and others til wasn't nobody hardly left for all the other pieces.

Something happened to me and I got sad and started thinking of being somewhere peaceful and away from all the things of my life I was tired of! I decided to take my children where they could meet their relatives before they was all dead. You know, have some background. That's when I saw Dearie B again. I spent more time with her than anyone else, cause the children had so many relatives they didn't even need me. I got caught up on her life.

Her mama, growing mighty old, had talked Dearie B into marrying a old, old man! The old man had had a job all his life and a wife some of it, so he had a house and car too. When his wife died, old and tired, he wasn't through living so he asked for Dearie B's hand and got it! Mostly because her mama wanted Dearie B to have a home for life if she died before Dearie. Somebody to take care of her child. Now, I ain't sure of her figuring cause that old man musta been Mama's age! Maybe she knew something that I don't!

Now, he didn't get no bad deal! Dearie was a good-looking, clean-living woman. A little sterner and quieter, but she could do all whatever he thought he wanted his woman to do! She was bout thirty-five or forty years old then. She was a good wife and loved her little home, her own to wipe, wash, clean, cook and sit on her own front porch in!

He was a ugly little mean man to me cause he wasn't nice to her at all! I don't mean he hit her or nothing, just wasn't nice. He treated her like she was a stupid child servant and he was Solomon's uncle! Marriage had changed her some cause she fussed and fumed a lot, behind his back, sticking her tongue out at him or giving him the finger! I wanted to laugh but couldn't, cause she was serious! You see, she was very religious too.

One day she showed me where she hid her money, saying, "One day I may leave this old bastard! He don't do enough for me! He too old and I'm too young! Lord yes! He don't do nothin but eat, sleep, have gas, and go sit in that car of his! Won't teach me to drive!" Another day she showed me through her closet, all her "fine clothes," she said. They just looked like regular old folks' clothes to me. I bet her mama helped her pick em out! She told me about a trip she and her mother had taken to some "Springs." She loved it!

We sat on the porch talking. She was just grinning and polishing the swing with her hands. "Oh I just love that travlin! We went on a long, long train! Had a dinner car on it! Oh, I just love that eatin out! And you can look through the window and see all them trees and skies and lakes going by, while you stir your coffee, girl!" She leaned toward me. "Me and Mama each had a glass of wine, chile! I keep it in the house ever since then. I'm grown and I can buy my own. I haves a glass ever now and again! Want some wine? Want a glass of wine?" I nodded yes and she went to get it while I sat on the slowly swinging swing and looked around me at the mellow, soft, quiet ending of the day. The lush greens of the trees and plants, the strong clear blue of the darkening sky, all looked so peaceful, so good, so huge. Then I thought of Dearie B's little heart and how little it took to make her happy and how little of that she seemed to have! She hadn't even heard of some things that would have filled her heart that was cut into little pieces for everybody else.

She came back with the wine, smiling like we had a secret. Then she frowned. "I ain't even gon to offer him none! He don't like me to buy it! So he don't need to enjoy it! Won't give me no money for nothing! I work a little extra for a white lady sometimes is how I get to save my own money!" We sipped.

"He don't even give me no money for flowers to take to the cemetery for my family and my friends neither. I gets em tho! He won't drive me there either, but I gets on the bus and goes to get my flowers, then goes to the cemetery. By myself!" She beamed.

We sipped and smiled at each other for a while. She leaned forward to confide. "You know, when I was on my trip with Mama?" I nodded yes while she covered her mouth with her hands. "A *man* looked at me!" She raised up to look into my eyes to be sure I understood this momentous thing that had happened to her. I looked deeply into her eyes and understood! She went on, satisfied. "A nice-looking, stranger man, girl! All dressed out in the latest style! We was there three days and every time I saw him, he looked at me and smiled! At me! He smiled!"

I was not joking when I slapped her knee and said, "Oh Dearie B! Chile! What you say!"

She laughed the happiest little-girl laugh and said, "I followed him, so he could smile at me." We both laughed. "He didn't have no wife as I could see!" She laughed gleefully. "Girl, if Mama hadn't been with me . . . I'da stayed three more weeks! Three years!" We laughed and rolled all over that swing. I wasn't laughing at Dearie B either, I was laughing with her!

She became serious all of a sudden and leaned her head back, closed her eyes. When she opened them again, she looked way out into the sky and said, "You know what I'm gonna buy me someday?"

I just got as serious as she was. "What are you going to buy someday, Dearie B?"

She frowned like she was thinking real hard. "A black lace brassiere and a pair black lace panties!"

It was my turn to cover my mouth with my hand and I wasn't acting. "Chile!"

She looked dead deeper into my eyes and said, "Yes! And a

black lace nightgown like them fast womens wear on the television! Yes, I am! And it's gonna be soon too!"

"Well, I declare!" I declared.

She covered her mouth to whisper tho there was no need to, her old husband could not hear good anyway. "He ain't *never* gonna see em tho! I ain't never gonna let him see none of my body in my fine lace." Dearie B weighed about 165 pounds now. I said, "How can you help it, he live here with you. You married!"

She looked at me with a frown. "Silly! We sleep in two different rooms! I don't never let him see me naked! We ain't done what you thinking of in nine years and we ain't been married but ten! The first year he just scrunched and rolled and act like he doing something . . . but I knew he wasn't!"

All I could say was, "I'll say!"

She went on. "I might not know all what it is, but I sure bet I know what *it* ain't!" I looked at her, wondering if she had been a virgin when she married. I don't know what she thought I was thinking, but she tried to explain.

"Well, if peoples kills bout it . . . and kings give up thrones bout it . . . people even die for it . . . it *got* to be better than what I know of that he do!" And I understood.

"When that old man die, I'll go on lots of trips! I'll do things he don't want me to do now . . . and things he *can't* do!"

I leaned back to look at the sky and think of Dearie B's life. She was getting on in age. You know, it didn't seem like too much to ask. What was she doing on earth anyway if she wasn't going to have something she wanted! Oh, I don't mean just sex. I mean all the living that goes with it! Love, stuff like that!

She was talking again. "I can't even have a cat or a dog or a bird! He say they dirty . . . have germs. He just don't love nothin."

She brushed some lint off her skirt that wasn't even there

and asked me abruptly, "You want to go visiting with me? See some of your other relatives?" I nodded yes and smiled. I felt like crying for some reason.

She smiled a little. "He'll take us since you here." I wasn't sure I wanted him to—he was very old, about blind, couldn't hear good, but he drove alright, I guess, cause we went. First we got some flowers and I thought, "Dearie B is a very thoughtful person . . . taking relatives flowers." Then we drove down a long, hot, shining street. You could see heat waves coming up from the pavement. People standing still and fanning. Walking and fanning. Sitting and fanning. Kids running through spraying water or holding hoses on each other, according to their place in life.

I ask Dearie B did she call the relatives to let them know she was bringing company. She leaned her pretty head back and laughed, "They ain't got no phone!"

He spoke, "You ain't told her where you goin, B?"

She stopped laughing on a dime and looked at him. "I told her we was going visiting my relatives and friends! She my cousin, not yours, so you don't need to worry bout what I tell her!"

We pulled into the cemetery, stretching out before us in all shades of green, grass and trees, surrounding hundreds of lonely tombstones. Dotted with flowers, real and unreal, that seemed to wish they were on somebody's shoulder or in a vase on some table instead of sitting on a tombstone in a graveyard. For some reason it was cooler here, hot but cool, you know what I mean? The sign across the gate said in huge letters, SUNRISE VIEW—PILGRIMS' PEACE CEMETERY and underneath, We Fill All Your Needs.

I didn't know what to say, so I didn't say nothin!

Dearie B said, "You can park out here. We'll walk on in farther, cause you don't like to come here noway! I got some flowers to put on your mama's grave."

He hesitated. "Now, B, don't be in there all . . ."

She cut him off. "Hush! We ain't gon be long! You shouldn't care noway! You don't never take me nowhere! I got to come out here for a party!"

I smiled and reached for the things she was handing me, broom, rake, large bag, whisk broom, things like that. It was beginning to feel pretty peaceful, sure enough. And pleasant! Wasn't too many mosquitoes or flies, and the view was nice, all green and everything.

Dearie B and I walked as she talked and told me about different tombstones and what time in her life they got put there. She knew some of the better-known people, so I got a quick history on the good and the dirt on the bad! All friendly. She whisked off a few stones of people she had liked when they was livin and arranged a few flowers for them. Then we arrived at a family-type plot, I guess, and she took the broom and busied herself and told me where to rake and whisk. She spread the blanket, later, and took food from the bag and a bottle of wine. We poured, drank and ate while she told me about every grave within a hundred feet!

"That's Uncle Greg over there . . . he left four kids here and a wife, but she made it alright. The kids got grown. She out here now, Melody, over there on the side of him. Over on the side of her is one of they babies who died at birth or right after. Sure was a nice woman, drank orange sodas all the time. See that brown stone over there, that was my friendgirl when we was growin up. Yes, she got sick, poor thing, sure was pretty . . . and love to dance! Oh, and you see that streaky white one? No, the one with the bird on it!? That was a beautiful woman. Sure was kind to everybody. We all loved her. Her husband shot her . . . while she was sleeping. Now that gray stone with the angel on it? He was anything but a angel, chile!"

I can't remember all she said, but I began to have fun. When we were through eating and drinking, we tidied up and read some of the funny stones she had noticed over the years.

She couldn't stand to see empty flowerpots so we spread all those flowers we had all over, even to strangers she didn't know, so you know I didn't! Then she took some flowers from graves that had too many and shared them with the poor, telling the first ones that God would bless them for sharing. She would laugh and say, "Some of these people ain't shared nothing while they was living, so now it's the last chance!"

I looked at Dearie B with new eyes. How in the world could I tell anybody one of my most pleasant days was spent at the cemetery with old relatives of mine and old friends of Dearie's, who were now my friends!?

Dearie B went off into one of her serious moments, looking off into the sky. "You know my mama is all I got left living. Ain't nobody close in my family left, sides you and you just a cousin. When she die . . . I don't know what I'm to do! Won't be nobody else. Ever. All my family be out here."

I reached for her to hug her, she patted my hand. "All through the years I done watched people I loved all my life just disappear away . . . one by one. Die. Gone forever. Can't say nothin' nomore. Can't kiss you, can't hug you. Til one day you look round you and ain't nobody there you knew in your life . . . nomore. When my mama die, I'm gonna kill myself and be buried with her!"

I squeezed her hard as I could and said, "I'll be your sister . . . forever!"

Almost three hours passed when Dearie B said, "We better hurry on back to *him*. Or the pilgrims won't have no peace and we might be looking at the sunrise from here tomorrow!" We reached the car laughing. He was mad so we drove home in silence.

Soon after I left, Dearie B's mother did die. I prayed for Dearie B cause she took it so hard. They put her in a psychiatric ward! Thought she was going to die! I didn't have the money to turn right back around and go, but I called that hospital everyday! I thought of that old, old man who was going to outlive life-loving Dearie B! I thought of the black lace brassiere and panties, the black lace nightgown. It was touch and go for about two months. Finally she was home. She was only my cousin, but she was my friend, I mean that! She had let me visit in her world and I had found it peaceful, pleasant, and exciting, small as it was. So . . . I borrowed the money and went to see her. She was stuffed with pills. They said she could be dangerous to herself or others because she was "mentally disabled." In the month I stayed I was able to get her off a lot of unnecessary tranquilizers. They were killing her heart!

She was coming round to herself and I finally had to leave. I had to get back to my job or lose it! She could look out for herself now. I took my last money and bought her them black lace things she wanted, showed them to her so I would know she would make it alright cause I knew she would want to wear them! They worked.

Her husband's family was trying to move in so if she died or he did, they would have a home. He was close to failing, too! Sometimes I saw Dearie B make a mistake and give him her own pills. At least I think it was a mistake.

I know a little something bout things so I took her to a lawyer and we got a will for him to sign leaving his wife all what he is supposed to! His relatives was looking things over, slobbering at the mouth! Made me ill! I went back home.

Next thing I heard, he had died. I called her, she said, "He was just old, but I'll take good care of him." Then there was silence. I thought about the pills.

Then she said, "Oh chile, all my familiar faces is gone now. Gone to the cemetery." She was crying.

I knew then she hadn't killed him. She would have held on to him just because he had been there all the time she had.

She went on, "I'm gonna join them pretty soon now."

I cried, "Oh Dearie B! Please!"

She said, "Oh, I'm not going to take my own life!" I could hear her smile in her voice. "I ain't wore this black lace gown yet!" I breathed relief.

The next few years she sold that house, bought another one. She didn't take the trips tho.

People began to call saying things like, "Dearie B is losing her mind. Didn't never hardly be sane noway!"

Then they began talking about a man. A *young* man, forty-nine or fifty-five years old, about Dearie's age, I guess.

In time I took another trip to see Dearie B. She had bought that other house right next door to the Pilgrims' Peace Cemetery! She grew flowers and went there everyday to take them to her mama. She was so close now, she didn't stay all day. She was content to look over from her yard and see her mama's stones. From some of the money from the house sale and his social security payments, she had bought two stones, one at the head and one at the feet! She kept her husband's grave clean too, but he had a smaller stone . . . one. She said, "He hated to waste money!"

She had a big, beautiful, golden striped cat, a German shepherd dog, and a parakeet in one cage and a canary in another. Her new family of love.

We sat on the porch in the new swing laughing and talking again. I didn't ask her bout the man, just waited.

She told me her life was happy.

She told me her life was full.

She told me, "I don't have to sneak and buy wine and good things to eat now. *He* brings things to me."

I asked, "Who is *he*?"

She smiled. "He is the caretaker at the cemetery. He is so nice. He been in a war. He don't have nobody in the world either. Cept now, he got me."

I asked, "How did you get to know him?"

She smiled sadly. "I'd see him and he was so sad all

the time. And mannerable. I started taking plenty lunch with me on my picnics for him to have some. That turned into him helpin me with my flowers and saving the best bouquets for me to spread round to the poor graves. I don't know when, but pretty soon he was doing things round the house here. Shoot! I don't know how to do the stuff this ole house needs!"

She covered her mouth with her hand and leaned toward me. "You still my best friend?"

I smiled. "I will always be your best friend."

She smiled and whispered, "I found out bout all that stuff we was talkin about! Remember?"

I whispered back, "Sure, I remember."

She whispered again, "*He* showed me!"

I asked softly, "Are you sure that's what you want to do with him?"

She stopped whispering. "Sure, I'm sure! Yes indeed! I'm not gonna let him stop! He loves everything I love! All my pets! He works at my favorite place! Takes care my favorite friends! My mama! He understand me when I tell him something!" She patted her hair. "He loves me! I wear my black lace every night! Done wore the one you gave me out! Got two new sets! I bought one, and he bought one." She laughed like a child-woman.

When I met him I could understand her more. He was a sad man, with a chance to be a little happy. He was kind and gentle with Dearie B. He was always patting or rubbing on her arms or neck or hair. They both like to eat so they were always cooking and playing like children. They both liked flowers, so her garden was full to overflowing. When I left there, I didn't worry. No matter what happens now, I'm satisfied! I always have her to think about when I get to feeling down with my life. I don't care what they say about her being simple. Simple truths are often the most necessary ones. I learned a lot from Dearie B.

Every Valentine's Day now, I get two cards. A half a heart from her and a ¼ heart from him! I laugh because they like laughter. . . . Dearie B and her man. They are my funny valentines. Even next door to the cemetery, I can never hardly wait to visit them again.

One thing I have learned! If Dearie B found happiness at the cemetery, we SURE can find some happiness for ourselves with the rest of the whole world out there!

When Life Begins!

This story is shaped like a Y. *Two paths lead to one road. I got to tell you two things, or stories, before I get to the main road where it all comes together!*

It's a old saying, if a thing start out too good it's going to end up bad . . . and if it start out bad, it's going to end up good! Well, old sayings been around long enough to get old, so it must be some truth to em! That's a fact and you can believe it!

In my mind is a boy named Wally born the ninth child to a man and woman who was friends of mine. Sad to say, he was the only one what lived! Out of nine!

They was country farmers. Don't know how they got hold of that forty acres they had, but I know it was some hard work done by somebody in his family and it had come down to them. Not far down . . . but it got to them! They both worked hard, not trying to get rich or nothin, just trying to make a living and survive. That's probly how come she lost all them babies! Doing that hard work, side by side with her man. He try to slow her down from the work, cause he love her . . . and she probly out there helping him, cause she love him! They coulda made it too, if living was fair, but no matter how hard they tried, they always end up owing at the end of the years . . . the white owners, you know, what owns the scales!

Anyway, when she had that boy and he lived, she took to doing things at home more, like washing for other people or baking things, to help out. He tried to do the farm work alone, waiting for that boy to grow up and help him. But a person can't do it all. Work in all kinds of weather, through all kinds of problems. There's many a thing you have to do on a farm . . . everyday! Don't know whether it was the hard work that killed him or if it was the constant, all-the-time disappointments bout always being tired and always getting nowhere and always being cheated by people who held the money! You gets mighty depressed, even sick, when people all the time treating you like a fool! Right in your face! If they don't make you hurt them, the hurt stays in you and . . . let me tell you . . . it will kill you! Killed him! That's a fact, you can believe it!

Now, Wally was a strange one. All the time things happen to him in a strange way. Like the day his daddy died was the first day Wally had found out he liked girls. He was bout ten or eleven years old. That age when little boys grin a lot around little girls. This girl was coming down the road in front of his house and he was out there tending his mama's flowers fore he went in for dinner. He had helped his daddy load the wagon to take to market and his daddy had just come back, so dinner would be soon.

Actually, he knew that girl came that way and went out there to work so he could see her better and maybe even talk awhile. Growing up, you know?

The girl had just reached him and was grinning back at him, cause she knew he had been watching her, with her little fast self! He grinned and said, "Evening." She smiled a big smile and said "Evening" back, then "What you doing?" tho she could plainly see he was working in the yard. He answered, "Fixin these flowers. Want one?"

"Ohhhhhhh sure!" she said, pleased. "I like flowers."

He was just handing one to her when his mama screamed and he froze in mid-handing!

"What's that?" the stupid girl asked.

He shoved the flower to her and whirled around to run to his mama's call, stepped on the hoe and the handle flew up, hit him right in the mouth and the blood spurted out, like he had been hit by a hammer or something! He was stunned! But his mama screamed again and jerked him out of himself and he flew into the house! Blood flying everywhere.

Life had finally handed death to the young old man who was Wally's father. Just lucky it was sudden and not no lingering, costly one! You know . . . cost him by the pain and cost them by the money they did not have. You might think it's terrible to think like that, but facts is facts and you can believe that!

Anyway, Wally lost his two front teeth. They was the second ones to come in, so there wasn't no more coming! And he had just started grinning at girls! Teeths important! You wait . . . you'll see!

They didn't have any money to spare and now that the husband was gone, the future looked worser than before! The first problem was how to bury him with no money. She, the mama, had two trunks she had brought with her when she got married, filled with homemade sheets and tablecloths. A hope chest, full of hope, old when she brought them. They nailed them together and fixed the lids so they would close and it became her husband's coffin to be buried in. Wally asked, "You gonna put them hope chests you love in the ground, Mama? They your favorite furniture!" His mama answered, "They still my hope chest. Your daddy blong to be buried in them. Sides, I can't make no coffin, can you?" He shook his head no. She went on talkin. "Well, we can't buy one, and if we could, it wouldn't be as proper as my hope chest for his coffin. Sides, what else I got to hope for?"

I believe that's when Wally made up his mind to learn how to make coffins, cause through the years he did learn and a lotta people used his coffins cause they was cheaper and they was all made like they was gonna be for his own daddy.

Tho they still had the land, the mother cut the land down they was gonna use. Not selling it, just not working all of it. She told Wally, "We will mostly work to feed ourselves. See that we have aplenty to eat. You a man (he was eleven years old) and you can do that. I'll wash and bake and knit and things, to buy the things we can't plant and grow. Nomore counting on nobody to be fair and make our life go. We'll make it go!" The boy sat looking at the floor, little quiet tears rolling down his cheeks. The mama standing looking out the kitchen window with the cardboard replacing the glass on one side, looking at the land. She turned to her son and asked, "You love me, boy? You love me, Wally?" He looked at her with love and said, "Yes, Mama, sho I love you." She took his hand and pulled him to her. "I love you too, Wally, from the bottom of my heart. We gon be alright if we just keeps that love!" And that's how their new life began.

Wally didn't go out to grin at that girl again. He was more tired and more grown-up. He was also shamed of his mouth with no front teeth. He had a powerful lot of work to do, helping his mama and surviving! It takes all your time, a day at a time, sometime, to just survive. Ain't no time for nothing else. But life don't hardly let nobody get away without nothing.

He was bout eleven years old, I guess, when he was chopping wood for ole Mrs. Farby one day. Now, Mrs. Farby had a daughter way too young for old Mrs. Farby to have, but who sposed to tend to her business but her? Anyway, he grinned before he thought, cause she was a pretty little ole brownskin girl, and at that minute the ax handle broke and the ax blade flew up and across his head, just skimming it a little, but it put a part in his head from his ear up! Not his ear, that was a little luck right there, but just above it. When it was healed, it looked like he had parted his hair and the part had slipped down and around a little.

Seem like the devil or something was always just waiting for Wally to grin at somebody so they could mess him up! Cause he stopped grinning or liking anybody out loud. Maybe inside in the quiet of his mind, but not out loud nomore! Well, with no front teeth and a crooked part in his head, he stayed to himself, helping his mama. They had a good big garden they sold some things from. Had a horse and a wagon he hauled people and things in for pay. He made coffins for the dead. She knitted for little babies and things and baked for weddings and wakes. They survived.

The mama was getting a little rheumatism and achy from losing all them babies and working in the fields and maybe from the loneliness of life too. But she kept on moving with life. Wally was laid up once for a little while, when he was shoeing a horse for another man who had his daughter with him. Wally must have grinned at her, cause the horse kicked and hit him on the side of the face, leaving a foot print there forever! He fell back from the blow onto a hot something and burnt his back too! Wally stopped grinning at anybody after that!

They was both getting older and sadder and lonelier. Wally got to be bout thirty-five years old and hadn't married or even had a girl far as I know of! You can blive me or not if you want to! Oh, they had each other and they loved each other, but there's somethings a man and a woman want to talk about and do that no matter how much you love your mama or your child, they just ain't the same thing! Ain't enough! That's a fact and you can believe it!

Now, we got to go back and start at the other side of that Y *and come down to the part where the paths meet and join.*

Some years ago there was another farming family, only these were tenant farmers. They was very, very poor and all the babies born to the mother lived. Was seven of em, mixed boys and girls. They lived in little brown clapboard shacks. Every little house was just like the other, wherever they moved. They was always cold in the winter cause these houses were full of holes and leaks in the roof. Some even had paper windows covered with cardboard. They always almost suffocated in the summers. Two rooms with nine people and a extra relative now and again generates a lot of heat to add to the heat of the sun!

The mama in this family was not dumb, but she was disgusted and sad. Not disappointed, that ain't the word, cause when she was born she didn't know nothing to look forward to noway! All she dreamed of, when she dreamed, was a piece of real furniture. Like a chair or a real bed to sleep in. New. All hers. And not to have to move so much. To stay . . . live someplace! Every day the sun come up was just like the last for all her years.

One of the middle girls was kinda retarded. Not quick to learn or nothing! Trusting. Not sense enough to be suspicious.

A visiting uncle, with no pride and no dignity in his manhood, spent a little time with her and played with her right on into the acts of sex and threatened to kill her if she told. She didn't have no sense to get too scared and so she told her mama, who just sat down on the broken steps and cried with the tears falling on her bare feet caked with the mud from the fields. She held her thirteen-year-old daughter and prayed she wouldn't get pregnant, but Satan heard the prayer and this being mostly his world and God looking a little farther down the road of life, she got pregnant!

The baby girl, named Marriage, was born by the time the uncle came round again. He tickled its chin and bounced it on his knee and said, "Who'd a thought that girl was messing around with boys!? Kids grows up fast these days!" and laughed. Mama sat on the porch in the dark and said she thought she'd make stew, meatless, the next day.

Dinnertime the next day, Mama told the men to sit out in the yard, it was cooler, and she would send a bowl of stew out.

She did that. After dinner, when most all who was sittin on the porch was gone on in to bed, Uncle said he thought he would turn in too. Find his space of floor, he said.

Mama said, "Wait a minute, I wants to talk to you," softly.

"Why sho," came his answer.

Mama looked off into the dark distance and said, still softly, "I know that is your baby, Uncle Tom."

Uncle Tom started sputtering softly so everybody else wouldn't hear, but Mama kept talking.

"I think you is less than a piece of snot! We let you stay here and she is your blood kin!" He started to deny and she said, "Hush! I'm going to tell you this. My chile ain't got the sense it takes to lie on you, so I know you lyin!" Silence was.

"Now," she continued, "I want to kill you but I ain't got the strength for it. And you ain't worth me goin to jail for and leaving the rest of my children out here to the likes of you."

He breathed easier.

She took a deep breath. "Ain't gon tell your brother, cause you all might fight and he get hurt and I can't lose his help round here." Her voice was soft, but it carried a menace. "So, I'm tellin' you this . . . this evening, in your stew, I mixed that baby's shit and some of mine and all of the spiders and roaches and caterpillars I could grind up! Just for you! I hope some of em poison!"

Uncle Tom like to threw up. "It seem so salty . . . different." He gagged.

"I put extra salt and pepper in it for you."

Silence.

Then she went on. "Everytime you come here that's what I'm going to do to your food, so you ain't never gon know what you be eatin. I'll think of new things too!"

"Ahhhh . . ." Uncle Tom started to speak.

Mama interrupted. "That's cause you put something in my daughter didn't nobody expect! And," she went on, "I'm going to hate you cause that's what you musta felt for us to do our chile, your own blood, that way. You got a baby mind or a baby wouldn't satisfy you! One day I may poison you or cripple you, like you have done her life!!"

Uncle Tom whispered, "Are you threatenin me to stay away from here?"

Mama said, "I don't never want to see you again! But I can't whip you your way, so I'll whip you my way! Come back if you want, but know that you got to eat my cookin! You can't cook in my house! And . . ." Silence a minute. "I would cry for joy to see you dead, cause a man with no God is a dangerous man to have round you!"

Uncle Tom looked through the dark to the road, sadly. Not sadly for what he had done, but for what was being done to him.

Mama got up to go in the house. "You know my tools now and you done heard my terms." She went on in the house.

Needless to say, Uncle Tom left that porch, going up that road, that night!

As that baby, Marriage, was growing up, her and her mama played like sisters stead of mama and child. Her mama was bout twenty-one years old now. That little Marriage was a sweet child. And I mean, a smart one! She looked after her mama like she was the one was the mama! She loved her grandma too and swore one day she was going to buy her a big bed all her own! Gramma would smile and pat her head, loving her back. Gramma wasn't feeling so well no more, laying on that cornshuck mattress on the floor. Marriage would lay there with her all day while the others were working in the fields. She would run get water, food, homemade medicine . . . things she could do, you know? One day, laying there holding Gramma's head in her lap, Gramma arched her back up in pain and screamed. Marriage wanted to run to the fields and call for help but Gramma wouldn't let her, held tight to her dress. She was in great pain but there was a lotta strength in them old hands yet! She gasped, "You all get on way from here!

Don't stay here when I'm gone!" Marriage cried, "Don't go, Gramma! Don't go! Pleassse, don't go!" But Gramma died in her arms on her lap.

Marriage had rolled up a few things in two rags for her and her mama. During the funeral when they buried Gramma, without a coffin, Marriage took her mama by the hand and slowly walked away with one little plant from the graveside in their hands. They had no plans for it, just wanted it! It was like taking some of Gramma with em! By nightfall, they was long gone! Never went back!

They slept in the woods or round the rivers, stealing food that was growing abundantly somewhere. Bathed in the streams and enjoyed everything like a game til winter came. Then Marriage said, "We better get a job, Mama, for the winter." They found one doing cleaning and washing work. Gramma had taught them to be clean, so they knew how to do that! Through the years that's what they did. Moved around free in the spring and summer. Find a job in some new town in the late fall and winter. They was honest and did good work so they found jobs easy enough. Everybody didn't want to be bothered with a child too, but no child, no mama, so they took them both and found Marriage to be a hard-working little help to her mama, then they was glad. Later on as she got grown, it was no trouble at all!

It was all fine til some man, older man, got to know Mama and wanted to take both of them home to live with him and Mama wanted to go! They went. Marriage bout nineteen years old then. She had never answered the men who tried to get her to leave her mama. Her mama was still like a child to her and she didn't want to leave her alone, even with the older man!

They made a home with that man til Marriage was bout twenty-eight years old or so. Marriage had almost left bout once or twice to go marry or run off to the North, but the man was not always kind to her mama, so she let people go on off down the road and she stayed home. Sometimes she had to bring in the food for them to eat, cause the old man got mean sometimes, talking bout having three mouths to feed when he didn't need but two! Only wanted one, either one! He would drink and then maybe fight. He had hit Mama once and Marriage had jumped right in on him with a big black frying pan. She lost two teeth tho. But he didn't pick on Mama no more when she was in the house, and she stayed close when he was drinking! They had no extra food or clothes cause he gave them nothin but a roof! Mama was getting old before her time and didn't want to leave, didn't feel well. They was just dirt poor! Worse off with that man than they had been without him!

One day, Mama died. Nobody knew from what. At the funeral the old man leered at her over that cardboard box Marriage had got from the mattress factory to bury Mama in. Marriage picked some plant from around her mama's new grave and placed it into the small paper bag she had already packed her 50¢ in. Her inheritance from her mama. They had always saved that same 50¢ piece, for hard times. She walked away from the grave, crying quietly, looked back twice, then kept walkin on away from that town.

The old man hollered after her, "Come on, let's go home! Come on, now! I'm your last relative! Come on!"

Marriage did turn and say, "Mr. Bubba . . . you ain't my last nothin!" and went on up that road . . . away.

Now! We at the fork of the Y *where the two paths join into one road of life!*

One day Wally was out tending his mother's flowers again, waitin for his dinner, when he noticed the woman walkin up the road by his house. When she got up to where he was, he could see she was kinda dusty and not too fresh, you know? Her blouse was torn, sort of, not from something sudden that happened to it, but torn with age . . . and faded. Her skirt was long to her ankles and the hem was hanging down on one side and looked like it was wet, like she had walked through some water or something. She was barefoot and her feet were a good sign. They were dusty but not dirty! You know, with the dirt ground in from never washing!? Her hair was thick with two braids tippin on her shoulders and she had a paper bag in her hand!

As she reached him, she slowed and looking at him she said, "I'm tired and I'm thirsty!" Well, this wasn't nothin to grin about so Wally didn't grin, just answered, "I'll get you some water." He started toward the house, then turned back and said, "Whyn't you sit down in my mama's chair there by the side of the house and rest?!" She breathed a sigh of relief and went on and sat. He brought her the water, then went and got a wet towel, saying, "My mama said bring you this towel." She took the towel with another sigh of grateful relief, wiped her face and arms, gave him the towel back, and took the water again, saying, "Thank your mama for me!"

Then she smiled at him. And . . . she had two front teeth missing!

Now, I don't know how anybody can get that happy in a second, but Wally did! He smiled right back, slowly at first, then *real big*! She saw his empty gums where two teeth should be and pointing a finger at him, she broke into loud laughter! Wally pointed back and began to laugh out loud too! That's how they became friends . . . laughing together, happily!

Mama heard that unusual sound of laughter out there and went limping out to see what was going on. Her heart thumped in her old breast to see her son looking happy! So when she looked at the young woman, she thought she was beautiful! Well, on account of Wally's laughter, don't you see?! Most mamas don't like a girl at first when she see her son do! Ain't that dumb?! Seems they ought to be happy he's happy! If he gonna pay dues for it, they's his dues and don't everybody have em? That's a fact and you can believe it!

Anyway, Mama asked her where her husband was and Marriage say she didn't have none! So Mama say, "Ain't you hungry? You look like you travelin a long way." Marriage answered, "I am hungry and I have been travelin a long way!"

Mama say, justa looking the woman over, "What's your name? Who your family? What's in that bag? Come on in the house!" All in one breath!

"Name is Marriage and I ain't never had one! My mama didn't have one, said I was her Marriage! She dead now and I don't talk about it! What's in this bag is 50¢ and a little rooting plant from my mama's grave. What I'm going to plant when I get where I'm going to be!"

"Where is that?" Mama asked as she went through the screen door Wally held open for them. Marriage let go one of them deep sighs she seem to have so many of between her smiles. "Don't know yet!"

The mama didn't even look shocked, like it was natural for women to have these problems! Just asked, "You ain't got no family at all? Where you gon to sleep tonight?"

"Somewhere I don't know yet," came the answer.

Mama musta made up her mind in a minute. "Well, you eat here and we'll talk and maybe you'll stay here . . . for tonight anyway. You can't be runnin around the roads at night alone!"

The preciation was in the voice. "Thank you, mam."

Mama turned to her son. "Take her out to the creek, she can bathe. I'll hold dinner down slow, then come on home and we can eat." To the woman she said, "Come on with me and I'll give you some towels."

Marriage followed her into the bedroom and Mama shut the door. Turning to Marriage, she asked in a firm, no-foolishness voice, "You got any man gon follow you wherever you going?"

"No mam!" came the answer.

"You got any disease?"

"No mam!" came the answer.

"You ever kilt or hurt anyone?"

"No mam! Not yet! To be full honest, I have wanted to!"

Mama smiled. "And you ain't married?"

"No mam!"

Mama hesitated. "You a grown woman, chile. I know you has had a man!"

The reply came readily. "Yes mam, two. I don't talk about it. My mama gone now and my life is brand-new ever since I been on this road today. Then I got this far and you gave me some water."

"My son gave you the water." Mama smiled. "He ain't married either! Go on, bathe, and here, put these on til we fix them clothes of yours!"

Marriage took the things, tears welling up in her eyes. "Mam, I just asked God what must I do with myself. I don't want to die, but how can I live? I ain't *had* nothin to love nomore and nobody to love me back nomore. Then here you come, being so kind to me. To me!"

Mama pushed her toward the door. "Well, if you got Him, you got aplenty family and a friend! The best one you can ever have! Go on! Go on and bathe."

Marriage followed with Wally leading the way, pushing briars and limbs from her path as she smiled at him, gums showing, and he smiled back, gums showing!

Wally said he would go away while she bathed and he would have! I don't blive he was no slick peek or nothin! Course I don't know, but I don't blive it! But she said, "No! Stay! I don't want to be alone!" So he sat down by the creek and stuck a twig in his mouth and watched her, looking away sometime to keep from staring, but staring in between! He was so glad to be round a woman, all to hisself, he didn't know what to do, what to say, so didn't say nothing!

I'll tell you something and I blive it's something we all know about! Bout life! Wally could see the air . . . felt it in his eyes! He heard the bird calls float out over the creek. . . . Saw the little insects going on about their lazy business. . . . The trees was there like they never had been before! The creek water flowed and bubbled over rocks and pebbles and played music for him! Sometimes it's called . . . Being Alive! Everything was realer! Wally was falling in *love*! And wasn't nothing hurting him!

Marriage didn't try to be sexy or nothin . . . maybe that's why she was. She just scrubbed and splashed, just natural. But she knew he was there! That's a fact, and you can blive it!

On the way back to the house, before they reached the clearing, he took her arm and asked her if she had ever kissed anyone before. She said she had. He said he hadn't, ever, and would she kiss him? She said, "Don't ask me cause I don't know how to say yes, just do it! I won't mind cause it's you and you been kind to me." He's a fast learner cause he just took her gently into his arms, a little clumsy. Well, what you expect? He held her close and they truly did look in each other's eyes trying to see what to expect, I guess. See, a kiss don't start when lips meet! It starts when you first think you want to kiss somebody! That's a fact, and I know it! Anyway, they got closer and closer, til she put her tongue out and rubbed it on his gums. He had washed his mouth at the creek and she was sparkling clean. He smiled joyfully and rubbed his tongue on her empty gums. She leaned back her head and said, "I think I'm gonna marry you, man, if you turns out to be nice like this all the time." Then he kissed her softly and held her a long time, til her stomach grumbled, and they laughed and went on to the house to eat . . . to dream, to sleep. Wasn't no fooling around cause they respected Mama! It was Mama who stayed awake, listening, til she dozed off, thinking of her life growing shorter every day and of her son's happiness.

The next day she told Marriage, "You can stay here if you want to. Just we all work and help each other, wherever we are needed."

Wally held his breath!

Marriage smiled. "I ain't scared of work! I worked all my

life! I been happier here in one day then I been for a hour in the last fifteen years of my life. I want to stay! I love you, Miz Mama!"

Wally let his breath out. "You think you will love me too?"

Mama sighed. "Wally that ain't the way you court, just straight out like that!"

Marriage said, "I love kindness."

Now it ain't no sense in trying to tell you everything you already know! Naturally one day Mama went to visiting her friends. Naturally Marriage was in the house cleaning and cooking, alone. Naturally she had been to the creek for her daily bath. Naturally Wally got through work early and come home to eat and naturally they kissed. Everybody knows what kissing can just naturally do, so Wally and Marriage made love for the first time, after weeks of looking and touching and little kisses and sleeping under the same roof. The bed was fresh with washed, unpressed, homemade sheets. The afternoon was springy, warm, not hot . . . cool, not cold. They lay there, face to face, looking at each other and smiling. Slowly he reached out and rubbed a small scar on her shoulder. Her face sobered, then smiled again. She put out her hand and gently traced the scar across his head. He sobered, then smiled again slowly. She raised up to kiss that scar and he raised up to lean over her and hold her closely. He told her it was his first time.

She said, "Not mine."

He said, "Show me what to do."

"I don't want no man I have to show what to do, Wally. It'll come to you. I don't know that much what to do myself!"

He asked softly, "Did the others . . . feel good to you?"

She answered softly, "One did . . . one didn't!"

He sighed. "I want to be good to you."

She sighed. "I love you. I think that's what makes it good."

And pretty soon, not too long, they was married! Mama rested back with a sigh, glad to move to the back bedroom and give her tired limbs a long-needed rest. She had a good son and she believed a good daughter-in-law. She was blessed! And Marriage was a good wife and daughter. Don't ask me why! Just time for that man and that woman's life to be good, that's all!

Time passed and Marriage didn't seem to get pregnant so they was able to save a little money. Wally even took on extra jobs for a year or so, and one day he told her he had a present for her and it turned out to be enough money to get her front teeth replaced. Said his would be next, then they could look like other people! She said, "I don't care bout no other people! They ain't doin nothing for me! I know what I want! Give me the money!" He gave her the money.

Early one morning she got up and drove herself to town in the wagon and came back with a BIG pretty golden brass bed and a pair of red satin sheets and a good factory-made mattress! She told Wally, "I didn't plan on the sheets, but there they were . . . and on sale! I started to get white ones, but country folks round too much dust, so red ones be just fine! We'll put em on the bed every weekend!" They just grinned at each other!

Them red sheets or that bed, one, musta did something to that man and woman cause almost right away she was going to have their baby, and a year or so after that she had another one!

Wally kept talkin bout the dentist again cause he said he didn't want his children to be shamed of him. Marriage thought about that and one day when she and Big Mama was preserving fruit, she took the wax from the jar tops and carved what looked like two teeth with a wedge to hold them in. She put them on, then carved Wally some and, it's a fact, you can believe it or not, them things looked alright! Only thing, you had to carve new ones every week! Cause they didn't last! Wally was happier, even tho he swallowed them a few times eatin dinner!

That Marriage was somethin! When she got a idea, it turned out to be somethin too!

Marriage had been watchin Big Mama and she knew she was lonely. Old folks get lonely too! Probly more! Nobody to talk to but them kids and they couldn't talk her talk! They talk children talk! She see Big Mama lookin off into the distance, like she just waiting to die or something! Marriage told Wally, "I want my children to have a whole family! A granddaddy too!" Wally told her right back, "Are you crazy? Mama ain't gone marry nobody nomore nohow!" She smiled. "Marriage don't have to be! I'll think of somethin!" And she did!

Marriage went round here and way off to places talking to preachers, lookin for a old man who could be useful and take care himself and was nice to be around but had no real home. When she found one of the few was around she took him home and made a place for him and gave him the rules of the house. Cleanliness and honesty and do what work you can! The old man was so happy to have a home. He took over the house garden work and made it larger. Added a animal or two to the stock and took over their care. He made hisself useful!

Big Mama didn't like it at first! She frowned and pouted and fussed, but as the old man made more and more things easier for her to do and made her a few nice things for her room, planted special flowers near her windows, and put a birdhouse there too, so she could see something all the time even without TV, her life changed. When the weather turned cool, Marriage put an extra bed in Big Mama's room and Harris moved in there. Mama didn't say a word, just told em how to put things. She wasn't so lonely anymore. They talked all the time and when their laughter burst out . . . Marriage and Wally smiled at each other. You could hear her asking where Harris was all through the day! She even took to going out and sitting, telling him how to work them plants, which he already knew, so they fussed some. Nice fussing.

She once asked Marriage, "What you think my friends think of a man sleeping in this house with me, even if we is too old to think of somethin foolish like sex? You think they think bad of me?" Marriage told her, with her hands on her hips, "They probly out right now tryin to find one just like him! Happy come before friends and people you know! If it's alright with your son and your grandchildren, they can kiss the backside of the man in the moon! Friends Hell! If they friends, they happy for you, not gossipin about you!" So that was that! Sex really wasn't no part of it, but they flirted the next ten years or so! That can be fun too, you know!

Now, I don't know what all else happened! I don't know how long everybody lived and things like that. But they was going long nicely when I moved away from there on the trail of some happiness for myself. All I know is there ain't nothin like love. Love and happiness! That's a fact, and you can blive that!

Without Love

I knew Totsy way back yonder when we were all kids. She was fast then and wasn't but eleven years old or so! Now, she was cute as a bug's ear, however cute that is, and always smiling, laughing, and running her mouth! She came from a poor family, like all of us, but that didn't stop her from looking at life, even then, like it was funny or something!

She would wear them little funny, hand-me-down clothes and shoes with the soles flapping sometimes, without a thought! She may not always have enough to eat, but she always had plenty boys for company. Boys loved her! Well . . . they was after her anyway. The other girls didn't like her too much. She was too popular! Most women always been like that.

We was kinda friends cause we walked the same way home from school together. I used to wonder what the boys saw in her so much and one day I asked her. She said, "You ain't had sex yet?" I gasped and shook my head no, and stared at this little person, my size, who know the secrets of *sex*! Why, she was eleven, no more than twelve years old! She went on just like it wasn't nothing! "Girl! you don't know what you missing!"

I drew my breath in and spurted, "You could get a baby! What your mama gonna say?"

She waved her hand at me, sweeping all that away. "I ain't got no monthly yet! Can't get pregnant! And my mama had a baby when she was fourteen, so she can't tell me nothin! She had her fun and I know why! Now . . . I'm having mine!"

Yes, she was fast alright! I was too scared for that stuff! My mama would have killed me if a boy even just hung around too much! But I guess her mama was still too busy. Anyway, I read books and was looking for my man to come on a horse and get me!

Years passed. Some of us girls did do it. Bout the time we was graduating from high school, some was getting married cause we were expecting little strangers. Well, that is the way most girls get married that I know! But Totsy wasn't getting married, wasn't getting pregnant, but was still getting a lot of the boys' attention. Her clothes were better, a little, cause she had a older man who owned a cleaners and he would give her the clothes nobody came back for . . . in exchange!

Now, the funny thing was, even tho all the boys and men hung around Totsy at times, none of em took her out in the daytime less they was new round here. But at night you could see her flying round in some car and hear her laughter in some corner of a party. She was wearing makeup now and long dangling earrings, even high heels! But nobody married her!

Later, maybe a year or so, she did get pregnant and told her mama. Her mama tried to get the boy's family to make him marry Totsy, but that boy said he would kill himself first! Said nobody didn't know whose baby that was! Said everybody in the school, and the county, and the state had done it to her! That it might come out in patches, all different colors and a nose, mouth, and ears that didn't match!

Totsy stood up there and cried like the child she had never been! Her mama took her home, shouting, "I'm going to the law!" They shouted right back, "Go head! We got witnesses!" They never did go to the law.

Totsy just lay round her house, listening to her mama low-rate her as she got drunk off that ole cheap gin. Totsy already smoked but now she took to drinking too! They both be drunk up in that house, shouting and cussing at each other! Didn't hardly hear that laughter ringing through the air nomore.

I know she didn't eat right cause her mama took all her money she got from the state and used it for herself! That baby she had was born made up of soda pops and cupcakes, chips, candy, jello, and a hamburger from the cleaners man, now and then.

Totsy was also crying a lot. The men who used to be round her like flies, was nowhere in sight. Didn't come round even accidently! Was no friends of hers at all! Shows them boys was only out for one thing!

I asked my brother about it all and he said, "They be back when she drop that baby! Everybody want something free, but it ain't free now, cause she gon have that mouth to feed! Sides," he went on, "if a man go round there now, people will think that's his baby!"

I thought a minute then asked, "Don't he want his own child? Why don't the father marry her?"

He snorted a laugh. "Don't nobody know if it's his! Sides that, don't nobody want to be seen with the town whore!"

I said, "She ain't no whore! She don't charge!"

He answered, "Been better if she had! Then she would have some money!"

I knew he knew something and I wanted to know it. "Wonder who it was. Who took her out bout that time?"

Men don't tell on each other, cause all he said was, "Nobody took her out! Didn't have to! Just sneak round after dark. Wasn't nobody gonna be seen with that girl! They like to tell each other what they did to her and laugh about it! They don't want nobody to see them with her, cause then everybody laugh at them too!"

I peered over my glasses at him. "Did you . . . ?"

He peered back. "Did I what?"

I hit him on the shoulder. "You know!"

He said, "That ain't my baby!" and got up and left me sitting on the steps.

Totsy had the baby and it melted into her family. Nobody talked about it anymore. She was soon up and out again, but she went with older men, farther out away from round here.

I was getting married bout that time and my life was full of Love and Romance. And yes . . . sex! I might not have waited til we got married, but we was engaged! I knew it was *him,* even if he didn't have a horse! We dreamed of a home, two children, a boy and a girl, and sleeping together every night and being together every day! Me and Syl.

We got all of it! But we worked so hard, so hard. We had our son while we was renting. Then Syl's boss heard of a house for sale, cheap, and when we saw it, I loved it! Just two bedrooms, but a could-be nice kitchen, bath, living room, and small dining room. It had a great big yard! I love a yard! And it had trees! I love a tree!

It took work and a lot of it, so we both worked. Syl rolled up his sleeves and took two jobs. We scrimped and sacrificed! I mean, we did without! But, little by little, over the years that house took shape. We would add a little here, a little there, and soon it was what we wanted! A home! I took off once to have my daughter, then went right back to it. We even had two cars. One raggedy, one good!

I had taken a extra job for the Xmas holidays at a department store and that's where I saw Totsy again. We were both a little plumper, but smiling about it! We hugged, cause I really liked Totsy! What she did with herself was her own business! She wasn't making me unhappy! She still had plenty makeup on and a real stylish hairdo. High, high heels with rhinestones sparkling everywhere! In her hair, her ears, fingers, and arms! She still had that beautiful big smile and gay laughter! We talked and I told her bout my children and she said that's why she was home, to see her son and bring him something, of course.

Totsy said she hadn't got married yet. Marriage was for fools! I smiled. She looked at my wedding ring and said she was going to settle down someday, but that a person has to have some fun first if the marriage was going to work! She fingered her rhinestone necklace and went on saying she had a very wealthy man in the city she came from who loved her, and lots of other men besides him who worry her to death, so that she was always at some glamorous party or club, drinking expensive Scotch and traveling to the very best places for vacations! All that . . . and more. That's when I noticed the sadness in her smile. And the restlessness in her eyes.

People were kind of noticing this bright, glittering woman and I became conscious of her clothes and jewelry. I quickly gave her my number and told her to call me sometime and got back to work, away from Totsy. I felt a small shame for being conscious of what other people thought. People was always moving away from Totsy. Then I thought of her son. He hadn't moved away from her, she had moved away from him! And that's probably who loved her . . . the one she left behind!

She called when she was leaving town—to borrow $20. Somebody had stolen her fare back to where she came from and she had spent all her money on her son. The cleaning man was dead, so there was only me to ask. I let her have $25 cause I understood she was broke. I thought about her rich man tho. Poor Totsy!

Couple years later, Totsy's mama died. I remember cause it was round the time of my daughter's wedding. Oh! It cost us so much! But it was big and beautiful and the joy in my daughter's beautiful eyes was worth it to us! Syl just beamed and went around saying, "My daughter!" all day.

Totsy came. Seems her mama's death hadn't been too hard on her. She came and had a nice time. Didn't bring no present but admired everything. She saw people she hadn't seen in so many years! She gave out her phone number a lot, to the men that is. They took it on the sly.

Her son had a wife and two babies, so Totsy was a grandmother now! Her son was a hard-working little man. Young man, I should say. Funny how, when you watch someone grow up, they stay little to you. Anyway, his wife stayed home with the kids while he worked. They were left the house when Totsy's mama passed. He had grown up in it, so I thought that was fair.

Totsy took up life with her usual self and pretty soon you'd see a man leaving early in the mornings. I didn't see it, but people was looking and eager to tell whatever they saw! I told them, "If you don't see Syl, I don't care who you see!"

Totsy came by my house to borrow $20 . . . again. I asked her, "To leave town again?"

She answered, "No, I want to fix Thomas a dinner. You know, his wife died a few years ago and he got a home and a job!"

I smiled. "Oh, Thomas is a good man, Totsy. I hope something works out!"

She said, "Hell, girl, Thomas ain't gon marry me! But I got to find somewhere to live cause that stupid-ass son of mine is trying to run my life! Talkin bout no company can stay all night no more! Ain't he somethin! Like he the one gave birth to me! I have to remind him that I'm the one the mama!"

I frowned. "It's a shame you have to remind him."

She paid me no mind. "I want to move anyway, since I can't make them fools sell Mama's house! We could all have some money!" She looked at me seriously. "Ain't some people fools?!"

I agreed. "Yes, Totsy, some people are fools." I looked at her closely and saw something else for the first time. She was not necessarily a misused sentimental woman, but an empty, selfish, no-thinking person! All the time I thought she needed a break! And she did! But . . . she took breaks and broke them! I guess. Oh, I don't know. This is, after all, a big strange world.

Anyway, I gave her the $20 and told her to keep it, don't have to pay me back. I knew she never had any money. I asked her once, "Why don't you take a job, over there where I work? They could use another person."

She laughed. "Honey, I can't get up that early!"

I said, "Work the late shift!"

She frowned. "Why you got to worry bout a job for me?"

I stepped back into my place and shut my mouth! But I told myself, "No more money that I work hard for is going to somebody who won't work for their own!" Now!

But back to Thomas. She bought the groceries with my money, Thomas ate the dinner that she cooked at his house. Then after taking her to bed, he took her to her house! I guess that was that, til he didn't feel like cooking again, or his regular girl was out of town again!

Didn't hear from her for a while, then one day she borrowed $20 from Syl. I wasn't home. She needed ticket money again! She left town telling her son, "You gon need me someday!"

All I said to Syl was, "You ain't gon see that money again, I don't think!"

He said, "I know it, but you seem to like her. She your friend, so I gave it to her."

I decided to get it clear now. I told him, "Thank you, honey, but I'll give the people I like what I think they should have and you give the people you like what you think they should have from now on, and we will miss a couple of big mistakes."

He looked at me funny and asked, "Did I do something wrong?"

I told him, "No, you got a good heart . . . but she don't!"

Well, he pat me on my hips and I smiled at him and we went in to take a nap. Now, we have been married a whole lotta years and been through a lot together. But, thank God, we still love each other. When we are in each other's arms, we are at home! A deeper home!

Well, the years rolled on and on. I stopped working. Now, I fool around my house and grow big, beautiful things to see and good things to eat! My days are full of grandchildren, sometimes. Club meetings take up a little time, my hobbies, and my friends. Syl and me take trips all over, different places.

On one of our trips to see our son I saw Totsy again. I was

driving through town looking for some Bar-B-Q for Syl, didn't see one. I stopped at a stop sign and looked around for someone to ask. I saw this lady sitting on the bus stop bench and pulled over, rolling the window down, and was shocked to my toes! It was Totsy! Now, we are way up in our fifties and I think I look it. Totsy was wearing a high, high stiff wig with hair everywhere, all down her back, and red! Still wearing them high-heel shoes with rhinestones and all that fake jewelry! Red fingernails and toenails too. One red toenail sticking out of the hole in the foot of her stocking! Eyeshadow smeared cause she had to take her glasses off to put it on, I guess! Lipstick the brightest, reddest, glossiest I ever seen, running in them cracks round her lips! When she spoke, her teeth clicked and a little saliva was in the corners of her mouth. She would wipe it ever so often and wipe her finger on her skirt, or a napkin. Some kind of lacy blouse with a dusty pink skirt, kinda short! Lord, she was a sight! Eyes running from alcohol, she leaned over through the window. "Geneva?" That's my name. "Geneva?"

Just outdone, I said, "Totsy!"

She laughed that gay laughter. "Girl, what you doin round here? Where's Syl?"

"Home, at our son's house. He got arthritis bad sometime."

She cackled. "Old age is somethin ain't it?! I ain't gon let it catch me! I look good, don't I! You look pretty good. What you doin driving round here? By yourself?" Then her smile changed. "Girl, you ain't getting smart and changing in your old age, are you? Come on in this bar and let's me and you have a drink! You got some money?"

I shook my head in wonder and laughed. "No, I'm not changing in my old age! And I see you ain't either!"

She cackled again. "No, girl!" She wiped the corners of her mouth and looked up and down the street.

I remembered my business. "Totsy, where can I get some good Bar-B-Q? Syl got his mouth set for Bar-B-Q!"

She leaned in the window further. "You still slaving for that old fool?!"

I got mad. "Do you know where the Bar-B-Q is?"

She looked up the street. "I would take you, but I'm waiting out here trying to catch my ole man passing by! He drives a cab and I know if I sit here long enough, he have to come this way sometime! I ain't seen him in a week! Ain't mens somethin girl?!"

I answered, "I don't know men the same way you do, so I don't know what you mean! And I am a woman, not a girl!" Then I smiled at her, cause why should I be mean to this woman with so little?

She asked again, "Want to have a drink?" and pointed to the bar close by. I started to go, just to talk a minute and try to see into this woman's reason for her life. Her style! I mean . . . what was different? In fifty years what was she doing today that she hadn't done thousands of times for the last fifty years? What had she learned? What did she think? When . . . did she think? When she was alone . . . laying up in her bed . . . looking at her ceiling, all by herself. What did she think of?

I sighed and said, "No, I better go on and get back to Syl." She looked at me with contempt, or, I hate to say . . . hatred. But it was something like that. Then, for a moment, she looked lost. She found herself and pointed toward a hole in the wall. You know, the kind of place that has that good Bar-B-Q. She started toddling off in them high-heel shoes, stopped and turned, saying, "When I see you, it ain't nothin but that ole devil callin me home again . . . and I ain't got no home! Ain't nothin there for me!" She started off again, turned again. "Is your phone number the same?"

I nodded yes. She passed her seat and went on in the bar. I drove off. She was back out there when I passed her with my Bar-B-Q on my way to Syl, or home, they both the same!

I guess it was round two or three weeks later when I got a call from Totsy. She said she wanted to talk to me and she was in town. I told her sure, come on and I'd fix us some lunch! She came. She still wore her hair and her nails were painted but the shoes were low heels and the blouse was warmer, quieter. She was sadder. After small talk, when the food was on the table and we were almost through eating, she took a deep breath and looked at me, saying, "You know, I have done give up plenty in my life . . . for other people . . . and I still ain't got nothing! I got a one room to live in, with a hot plate! No money!"

I poured her some soda.

She went on, "I got a man, too." She smiled sadly. "A young man, thirty-eight years old." She fingered the tablecloth. "He drive a cab. But he got a young girl bout thirty-five years old trying to get him from me!" She looked out the window. "Now, I'm too strong for that! I done forgot more than she will ever know! But . . . but . . . I'm tired. Geneva, I'm just tired. Don't feel like fightin for my love, nomore."

I didn't know what to say, but was glad she had started thinking bout her life and her future. Don't care how old you are, you got a future til it's all gone!

She spoke like the words were painful, like how it hurts when you want to cry, in your chest. "I get up in the mornings, wash my face . . . and when I look at myself? I just cry sometime. My looks is going away. Then what happens? What I'm gonna do?

She stopped talking a minute and blinked her eyes real fast, like you do when you trying not to cry. I reached for her hand.

She pointed to her feet. "Them heels hurt my feet! And oh Lord, my back be painin' me so bad sometime it's all I can do to get home to my room!" She lifted the hand I was holding. "Sometime I pick up something in my hand and I can't hold it! I can't! No strength! Doctor say it's liquor, but I don't drink that much! Sometimes I'm so sick I feel like dying . . . and my man have to work and can't look after me! Sides, I can't tell that young man I'm sick! He will think it's because I'm old! I can't tell him that!"

I held her hand. "Well, what you gonna do, Totsy?"

She held my hand tight. "I keep tryin to think of a future, but I can't think of none nomore. Girl, Geneva, I ain't even made love in two weeks!"

I thought of the fact that I hadn't either, but at least it was there if I wanted it! I said, "Totsy, is that all you going to think of *all* your life? Is when you make love?"

She looked surprised. "What else is there sides love in life?"

I shook my head. "There's all kinds of love. You concentrated on only one! You know, you got to wrap something round love besides a vagina!"

She thought that was a joke for a minute, then was serious. "But the sex got to be good!" she said. "Geneva, you know something bout life after all, don't you?"

I couldn't believe it, that this woman thought I was dumb! I asked her, "Sex plus sex equals what?" All she did was laugh! I said to myself, "You are stupid." Not unkindly tho.

She was tired of this "game," so she said again. "I'm tired! I'm tired and I'm sick! My mama used to tell me there'd be days like this!"

I agreed. "She was right!"

She grabbed my hand and looked dead at me. "I'll be better soon tho! I just need to rest! I caught a bad cold being out in the rain! Didn't have no coat, it was in the pawnshop!" She coughed and looked at me.

Syl came in then from his little league basketball group and grabbed a beer and left. She spoke to him very formally and watched his beer til it was out of sight.

I asked her, "You want a drink? A beer?"

She smiled. "A beer is bigger! I'll take a beer!" I gave her one and while she sipped it, she set her body and her mouth and spoke.

"Geneva, my son said if I come home, I have to stop drinking so much and I don't really drink much. And that my man could not come here to stay with me! That no man could even come and spend the night! In my own mama's house that is part mine too! I'm tired and I need to rest . . . and get better!"

I'm a fool so I waited, feeling sorry for her a little. She went on, nothing could have stopped her.

"So, I'm asking you. You have always liked me, been my friend. I need a place to stay, only for a while, just til I get my health back! A month or so?"

I looked at her and knew it would be way more than a month or fifty months and she still wouldn't have her health back! Cause she meant youth and her youth was long gone! I looked at this woman, this person who had made all her own choices, did her own thing just the way she wanted to! Loved sex and devoted her life to it! Waved houses and children to the wind! Doing her thing! No sacrificing for nothing for her future! Now, she wanted to enjoy the things I had sacrificed for, for my future!

"Totsy," I said, "I'm sorry. All what I have, we have worked and planned for, the hard way. We did without and you did what you thought was best for you. You ain't blind! You saw old people! You saw sick people! You knew you was human and if you lived long enough, rainy days was coming! You didn't get ready! Now you want to live off my ready!

"Now don't go talkin that same ole shit!" she snapped.

I stopped her. "It's that same ole shit you asking me for! Of mine!"

Silence a moment while she searched for a way and I found one.

"I ain't no fool, Totsy! You ain't no fool! We both know I didn't have no more strength or beauty than you when we started out. I didn't use my strength, and Syl's, all these years to make a home for you to have when you got old! That was for you to do for yourself!"

"But I'm sick!" she wailed. "What's a friend for?"

I took another breath. "You ain't even been a friend to yourself, Totsy! I don't want your problems! Why should I take your problems and ain't had none of your fun gettin em?!"

She smirked. "Oh, I see! You jealous! That's it, jealous!"

I laughed without a sound. "God bless the child that's got his own!" I got up and went into my room, not knowing why I was doing it, but I got $50 out of a drawer and took it in and gave it to Totsy, saying, "Now I gave you all the other money you wanted to borrow! This I'm going to lend you! I don't want to hear from you bout nothing til you got my money to pay me!" She took it. I knew she would. I knew she would never be able to pay it back so it was a goodbye gift. My mama always said when you get tired of being bothered by certain people, lend them some money! You won't see them again!

I do see her sometime and wave. She live with her son and he's the boss. She lucky to have that son! She's changed. The sparkle is gone. Totsy gave it all away! She liked sex whether there was love or not. And like my mama say, "God is love . . . and without love, there is nothing at all!"

Speaking of the Lord, you know, Totsy goes to church all the time now. Either somebody over there she likes or she truly got religion! I don't know cause she don't speak to me no more! You know another thing, I still like Totsy, just something about her. I don't know.

I still got my own problems of making survival, so I just take care of them. Syl worked hard and is sick with his arthritis now. I don't feel all that good all the time in these old-age times. But we expected all these things. We got ready best we could. We prepared for it and here it is!

Anyway, now, I'm going in here and rub Syl's balding head. Maybe later on we'll take a nap after we eat his favorite dinner of steak and have a glass or two of wine, in our own house with our own things around us, just like we wanted. And when we get to where there is no more sex, and we may . . . we will still have all the love we wrapped around it!

The Watcher

I have always, always, tried to do right and help people. It's a part of my community duty and my duty to God. But I can tell you right now, you don't never gets no thanks for it! For nothin you do! My life ain't been no bed of roses either, but I still takes my time to do for others. Not one person has thanked me!

I ain't feared of nothin but God and white folks! God, cause He is the boss! White folks, cause they runs this world and they don't know what they doing! Don't talk sense! You ever hear them shows on television where they talkin bout Law and Order? They use up all them big words in them long sentences and ain't said nothin but somethin to help themselves! Seems they dance all around the least thing to answer everything and then the show be over and they ain't settled nothin! I try to holler and tell em but they don't want to listen to nobody! But I do, I *do* try to help other people as my religious duty.

Use to be a big ole fat sloppy woman live cross the street went to my church. She had a different man in her house with her every month! She got mad at me for tellin the minister on her bout all them men! Now, I'm doin my duty and she got mad! I told her somebody had to be the pillar of the community and if it had to be me, so be it! She said I was the pill of the community and a lotta other things, but I told the minister that too and pretty soon she was movin away. Good! I like a clean community!

Take that woman over there up the corner, cross the street. Now, she got five kids with that husband she got and she thought they was happy just cause they was well-fed and all, but there's more to life than that! Now I knew her husband was foolin round with that Dorothy woman on the side. Her house joins theirs from the backyard, but on another street. I went over there tryin to help her by tellin her all about it, but she got mad at *me* and told me to get out of her house! Well, I left cause I know it's some people you can't do a good turn for. She not only put me out, she put *him* out! I don't know where he went, but I do know what I was talkin bout cause I seen him with my own eyes!

See, some nights I go up there to a place where people park in the dark. I be lookin to see is my daughter up there or is she wherever she sposed to be. I seen this car just a bouncing round in the night. It looked like that man's car so I said maybe he was sick in there or something and maybe I better do my duty as a human being and help him! But when I shined my flashlight in the window, I didn't see nothin but booty flying, chile! He wasn't sick! He had plenty strength to look up and cuss me all kinds of names! Me, a religious woman! Trying to help him! Anyway, I left there and came straight home to ease my heart and first chance I got I did my duty and tole his wife! He done made all them babies at home and he out there in the car tryin to make some more! Honey, I don't know about some people! But that ain't all! After she put him out, she had the nerve to come to my house and ask me for some money for food for them kids of hers! They ain't mine! I told her I didn't have nothin to give nobody and she better put the police on that busy behind of her husband's! She didn't speak to me no more, but I did my duty and I don't care! Wasn't too long fore they got back together and they moved. One thing I can say bout this street, people always moving. I been here longer than anybody!

Now, there was a man and a nice woman use to live on the side of me. He was a really heavy drinker tho. He didn't never fight his wife, but he threaten to sometimes. He brought his pay home and all, all of it, his wife said. I don't know where he got money for that liquor from, but he did. I liked his wife and felt sorry for her so I called her mama and told her what her daughter was going through, then I called his mama and told her what kind of son she had. She was a fool cause she hung up on me. Then I called Alcohol Anonymous and told them to come over to his house, like I was his wife, cause I know she never would have the grit to do it. Then I called the police and told them to watch out for his drivin and gave them the license number, all that, for his good and her good! Well, one night right after that, she was cryin when he really had done hit her, (I knew he would one day!) for callin' all them calls! So I told her that he should not beat her cause it was really me tryin to help her! She jumped up and you see this scratch right here cross my whole face, don't you? Well, she put it there! Just for me tryin to help her! They done moved away now. Good!

Oh, I have my troubles tryin to help people! My cross to burden! Just at that time my daughter had to go to the hospital! Seem she had tried to abortion herself, right there in her room, and she was so quiet I didn't notice nothin about it and she was bout to die when her daddy noticed and took her on to the hospital. That was on the night I usually go to check that dark parkin spot for her, so she was already in the hospital when I came home . . . and had to rush over there! A good person's work is never done, I tell you! When she was better, I ask her when she got that baby, how did it happen? She say, in her own room! Her own room! When I be out doin my errands of mercy and also tryin to protect her, that's what she do to me! Now, my son didn't give me that kind of trouble. He just stay in his room or go out for a little visit sometime. He go to high school and work part-time, a good young man. When he wasn't readin, he be sleepin when he is home. No trouble at all!

Now about that time, too, the couple what lived over on the other side of me, the woman had just got herself a job downtown there in a insurance agency. They was always kinda doing poorly with money. But when I seen she was gettin some new clothes and going out of that house every day looking prettier and better, I knew something was wrong somewhere! She was getting another man! Don't you see? Well, I changed my insurance over to the company she was working for and I commence to go down there to see about it, and I would see her sometimes with a pencil and a pad in her hand. Well, that pencil and pad didn't fool me! I'm too smart for that! She would go in a room with a man and close the door! Close the door! Honey, you can't fool me!

Well, I was out in my garden one day after that, did a lot of work in my garden that week, and finally her husband came out with the garbage and I told him he better protect himself cause of what was happenin in his own house under his own nose. Well, I thought he had some sense! I heard them arguing that night and I heard the gunshot too! He had done shot her! I prayed for her tho and so she didn't die. But she moved on away when she came out the hospital. I could have told that man that she was gonna leave him when she got that job! Anyway, she left. Now, I didn't mean for all that to happen, bullets and everything! Sometimes you can't help people, cause they ain't got sense enough to know what to do! And I shouldn't have helped him anyway, cause he don't know right! That was his baby my daughter was gettin rid of, I found out!

That's another thing, bout that time my daughter ran off with one of them card-playin double-dealin suckers that hang around the Buzzards Nest nightclub. She gone now. I don't know where. After all the protection I tried to give her! I still go on my midnight trips to the parkin place, done got in a habit of lookin after my chile! But one thing I can't get over is my daughter tellin me fore she left, I didn't pay her no mind . . . no attention, that she couldn't talk to me! Now one thing I do know . . . I was a good mother to that child! Telling me that! But God don't like ugly and one day she be back, needin me!

Now, the worsest thing was the woman what lived right directly cross the street from me. She was a nice enough lookin woman, but she wasn't married and she always dressed real nice and she worked. I never did see no company coming over there cept her mama or somebody like that, but I knew something had to be going on wrong! A single woman!? Lookin that good and all!? Don't you see? Well, ain't nobody else on this block gonna do it and somebody has to care about the community and all, so I took to watching over there all day and didn't never see nothin so I took to stayin up watchin that house all night! I wished I was two people so I could watch at the back of her house too! I'm a very steady person, my mama used to always tell me that, so I was steady on my job. My husband used to call me to come to bed. I told him no, I had a job to do. I knew what he wanted anyway!

Well, six months passed and still I ain't seen nothin! I figured it must be happening when I had to get some sleep, so I made my husband watch when he was home and I slept. He didn't like it at first but he soon understood what I meant, least I thought so. Do you know what happened? They made friends! In a month, they was talkin! Then everything was interrupted! My son died! From an overdose of heroin, the doctor and the police say. Right back there in that room! In my house! He was so quiet, sleep or readin! A mother can't see everything. And we had no sooner buried him, my husband and me, when my husband left me and filed for his divorce! Now HE the one I see going in that woman's house across the street! And he told me they was gonna get married! And move. He kept sayin they was gonna move! Lord, lord, lord, what must I bear?! I been a good wife and a good mother, all my time was given to the betterment of my family and see here what I done got! Ain't no thanks in this world!

Well, I just got a job to do, that's all! To hold up my community! When a lady, bout my age, moved in next door to me where that man had moved from, I told her about this world and this community and told her she could help me clean out the bad ones. But she said, "Leave it to God to judge." See that? Her religion don't mean nothin to her! Leave it to God! I am one of his deciples! I have the miraculous gift! I do His work! She told me I was a fool! And I was wrong!! Well, after I jumped on her and beat her up, yes I did! Yes I did! You don't talk to no deciple like that! Anyway, after I beat her behind, she told my minister, the same one I used to talk to. That man had nerve to open his mouth and tell me she was right and I was wrong! I knew he was the devil then! I almost quit goin to his church but I changed my mind. I don't sit up in the front no more tho, I sit way in the back. I ain't through! I'm watching her, that lady next door. I'm watching that minister too! There is a sin there somewhere! I don't take much time to sleep now, ain't nobody here but me, noway.

I stay here . . . in this window, on my job. . . . Watching!

At Long Last

Julia is a friend of mine, has been for many, many years. I remember when I first saw her, we were children and she was standing there, twisting her dresstail, sweating in the sun with the hair grease her mama used running down the sides of her head, watching the other children play. She was a quiet girl, thoughtful and shy. Not ugly, not good-lookin, but clean. I played hard and looked it, clothes always goin every which away. I talked loud and bossy and I got my way. For some reason I took to Julia. Just liked her. Well, she wasn't no trouble and would do anything she could to help you if you needed it.

We all grew up in a little bitty town where all the families were far more poor than middle class, but we were not dirt poor! Whatever that means! We had sufficient food and clean clothes, store bought or not. Of course, we grew our own food mostly and made our own clothes. Just was raised to be as self-providing as possible. Country people is mostly like that.

Julia had a lot of fun playin after I made her get involved with us. We played the kind of imagination games children play who have no toys. But she was a very serious girl. Her mama and papa were strict and demanded respect and had dignity, so Julia respected marriage and the family. That's why later she would never dream of a divorce or anything else *they* hadn't done.

Julia fell in love, puppy love, some would say. Puppy or not, she loved Stanley with all her heart. She loved the ground he walked on, as people say. She could have eaten it . . . and anything else he touched! She didn't tell him tho, just stared at him all the time, watched him whenever she could. She would stand there in the little schoolyard, sweat running down through the grease on her head, lean against the porch of the school building, and watch Stanley steady. Sweet Stanley, as he was sometimes called, cause most all the girls was sweet on him. He knew Julia liked him and teased her, laughing about it, cause he wasn't thinking bout her. No! No! He liked them long-haired high yellow . . . like himself . . . like myself, but I wasn't thinkin bout him, don't like his type, wouldn't give him a gnat's butt to sit on! I already had who I liked anyway!

School-leaving time came at different times for different children, according to the needs of their families. Julia's mama wanted her to stay in school. She knew her child would need that education for whatever future she could scrape up! Julia did finish high school, maybe cause Stanley did, but somewhere in between lessons Stanley must have gone too far with his teasing. Julia became pregnant and, of course, no doubt about it, Stanley had to marry her. Both families agreed wholehearted. Only Stanley was mad cause his eye was on another sparrow in the town close by . . . Alma. Well, he married Julia but tried to keep on with Alma, who slapped and teased him, laughing at his misfortune until he tucked his tail and went on home to his wife. Who knows? In time he mighta started loving her. She was a good little wife and a good mother. Clean, obedient to the laws of her upbringing.

Stanley became a insurance salesman and later added real-estate selling. That made them have to move to a bigger place where more people were and more houses to sell so he could make a better living for his family, which now had grown to two children. A boy and a girl.

Julia was happy but . . . was not happy . . . all at the same time. She would sit in church with her children, fanning, cause she was still sweating through the grease in the neat parts in her hair, thinkin about life and love. She would look at the other ladies and wonder how their lives were. How their nights were . . . their lovemaking.

You see, when Stanley wanted to make love . . . sex . . . he simply crawled up on top of her, whether she be sleep or not! I hate somebody to do that to me! Act like I'm a old dog layin there waiting to be done to! Makes me mad! Julia took it. Do what he had to do and roll off and soon be snoring. Like he was mad at her, but not too mad to get his good feelings! He never kissed her. She kissed at him, cause he would laugh, friendlylike, and push her away. Now, she had seen her daddy and even other men pat their wives on the hip or back with affection. She wanted that. Stanley never did that. Other people grabbed their wives' arms or hair . . . Stanley never did that. Personally, I think Stanley was a fool! He don't know what he missed with all that love layin beside him, lovin him. You hear people talk about gettin a "strange piece," somethin they ain't had before? Well, Stanley had one right in his bed up til the day he died . . . somethin he never did get to!

He was good otherwise tho, I got to give him that! He gave her much respect, even called her "Mrs. Wills," never just "Julia." I guess he said, "Well, you wanted that name, so there it is!"

Anyway, they moved to the city and Stanley did all right and, I got to be honest, he gave Julia most all his money. He was a good provider! She didn't want for nothing he could give her that cost money. If he fooled around, which he did, she never got to know it. Or, if she did, she never let on. Not to my knowledge and I was and am her best friend. She loved him as before tho, maybe even more. But she was the loneliest woman in town. Being lonely never even flickered through my life. I coulda been busier than I was, but I ain't no fool. You don't know how long you may live!—save some . . . make it last!

Everything Julia did, she did it thinking of Stanley. Get up, think of Stanley. Work, think of Stanley. Wash, think of Stanley. Cook, think of Stanley. Shop, look at the time, read, go to the doctor, bathe the children . . . think about Stanley! All the time. He was her whole world . . . and them children, of course, cause they was Stanley's children. Another man wouldn't cross her mind for no reason in the world! The children picked these things up and looked upon their mama, not as a slave exactly, but as a servant! For all of em!

Now, naturally, time passed. Stanley provided his family with a fine big house and a beautiful car, with Julia taking care the money wisely. When he got tired of having to take Julia wherever she had to go, he taught her how to drive and got her a car too. She lost those few precious moments with him. He dressed his family nicely. He just hated to look up and see his little girl, sittin or standin somewhere, sweating through the grease on her head, water running down her cheeks and the braids sitting on her shoulders. Julia had everything, but she was still the loneliest woman in town and Stanley still made sex-love in the same relief type of way . . . His relief!

In time the son married. Done made somebody pregnant that he didn't want. Julia made him marry her after she found out she was a nice girl from a nice family. Stanley didn't say nothin! That boy stayed with that girl long enough to make another baby, then he left her. I think he been married three or four times now, til he got a woman keeps her foot in his behind. That musta been what he was lookin for cause he kept her!

The daughter just kept on going to school, then college, then work. She was quiet and smart. She was going to pick her own husband, so she was taking her time, she said. Finally she married a man with a good job and she was off to live her life!

Julia had only Stanley to love and wait on now and she did just as always. Everyday. Every year!

Now, sometimes, them that's got, keep getting. So Julia got Stanley's mama, old and in need of care, to take care of. Stanley's family thought Julia had more time than they did for the old woman. Julia moved her right in, without a break in her step! Then she got her own mama to take care of cause she was getting senile and needed help. Father was dead and gone, and brothers think sisters should be the one to take care of old parents, sometimes, most times. Now, this took up Julia's life from bout the time she was forty-six to when she was bout fifty-seven or fifty-eight. I forget cause I don't pay no tention to age, specially somebody else's. Then, one died, her mama I think, and a year or so after that funeral, the other one died. She was alone with Stanley again.

Stanley had always been a drinker and smoker, but now he stayed soberly drunk all the time. Something went wrong with his glands and after the operation even the sex was gone. Julia missed it and didn't miss it cause their lovemaking had dropped way down to once every couple of months. But she always kept, still had this *great huge* need to be loved. *Loved!* She laughed at herself tho, a little, cause she was fifty-eight years old or so and she knew loving days were behind her. She cried too sometimes, when she thought of the lovin she had missed. She knew about that stuff cause I shared my life with her, some of it, cause you ain't supposed to tell nobody everything! She had never felt it when Stanley made love to her. *Never!* Oh, she felt happy in her heart cause she loved him and that was the only way she could put her hands on him! Even after all these years! But whatever he got in the end, when he moaned and sometimes hollered out . . . she never felt that . . . never got that feeling.

Stanley began to fall out different places. He had to take to the bed for good, and began to wet that. Julia never let up a minute taking care of him. Their grown children never came hardly, and when they did they told her things *she* ought to do for him. They rather do anything than give her a few hours rest. Now, he had done worked hard for them all his life, but they didn't have time for him . . . or her . . . when they needed help back. Children . . . we don't never know how they gonna turn out. The sweetest little babies and younguns turn out to be the biggest pains sometimes.

Anyway, Stanley lived, well, lingered, round there another four or five years with Julia ever on her job as a lovin wife til he died. He got the best funeral could be and she went home alone for the first time in sixty-five years. Sixty-five years to have a day to yourself! She grieved. Grieved for all that grief! She missed him! Well, what can I say, he was all she had ever known. I stayed around with her and talked to her much as I could. Well, that's what a friend is for.

One day Julia woke up and there wasn't anything to do for anybody but herself! And she liked it! She lay there in bed, listening to the radio. Then got up, fixed her breakfast and ate it leisurely, looking out the window at her garden, enjoying herself. No calls to answer, no sheets to change with number one or number two on em! No special dishes to be cooked for the sick and even fed to them. No doctor to be called or visited. Just herself to think of. Was a good, real different feeling!

She gave all the clothes away, along with all the things she was never going to use again. She joined ladies' clubs, travel clubs, and took to going out to expensive dinners once in a while with a few friends. Her life was better and brighter! She had a nice automobile and a lovely house and money in the bank! Now! She had earned every bit of it!

Then . . . her son moved his family in. Didn't want his mama to suffer alone, he said. Huh! Him and his family didn't have a home cause his wife wasted every dime he could get his hands on! They expected to eat when Julia cooked her dinner. If she went out to eat, they ate her food! The daughter-in-law never had worked, but the son stopped workin, not feeling well or something. He layed around thinking of new ways to borrow money from his mama he was never going to pay back! Well, it was some of her fault cause when she was raising him, she was actin like a servant to his daddy!

Then the daughter, who was kinda unhappy with her husband, thinkin her brother was making out too well, left her husband and moved in with her two children. She was lazy when she was at her mother's so Julia had to do all the cleaning. After all, they thought she was the servant, I'm tellin you! And that's what they wanted again. She felt because they were her children she owed them, so she did it. But she caught herself being awful tired, not just her body, but her mind too! She looked up and she was unhappy, again. A couple years of this and quite a few thousands of dollars gone in loans and other things her family needed, and she was sick and tired of them all, told them so. Told them to leave and be on their own. But they told her she owed them, that daddy had worked for them too and this house was going to be theirs someday so why should they leave?! There was always some argument going on in the house, sister-brother, brother-wife, wife-sister. No peace. *None!* No one had any money to speak of but Mama, and it was going fast!

I wanted to kick all their behinds but decided to settle for making Julia come visit me. I live in another town now. She needed a rest and some fun. Yes! I still have fun. Ain't gonna let no woman's child, mine included, ruin my life! May not have but a little left, but it's all mine! I told Julia while she was visiting me, "You are sixty-eight years old and done gave up your life already! You been a good daughter, good wife, good mother, and as if that ain't enough, now you just a good thing! Why are you scared to live the rest of your own life like you want to? Need to?" Oh I talked to her. She is my friend! It was making me sick!

Now, I have plenty friends, men and women. We play

cards, bingo, and other games. Some of us play music so we get together and do that. We go to concerts, plays and ball games. I like my life! I planned lots of things when Julia was here. On one of them music occasions, Clint, a seventy-year-old friend of mine, took to Julia. Took her to dinners, to the movies and kissed her too! She let him cause this was something she had never had, never dreamed she ever would have now, and here it was! Late, but better late than never! He even tried to feel her breast near the time for her to go back home. She didn't let him, but she liked that he had tried! Now, you may think that's terrible, but you be lonely for sixty years, wanting something you never got and see what happens when you get a chance to get it! If you think you wouldn't take it, then you don't deserve it anyway! Even a dog and a snake like affection!

Julia talked to me about Clint and everything. I told her, "He's a nice man. Likes nice things, food, clothes and ladies. I hear he is a strong man and I blive what you need is somebody to tip your basket! He ain't poor neither! He is not lookin for a home to move in and die! He got one!"

Julia didn't hear nothin but bout the basket. She said, "Tip my what?"

I said to her, "Girl, you told me it ain't never been tipped!"

Julia blushed, at her age, saying, "We are too old to even think of things like that!"

I told her, "We may not need as much, but everybody needs love. If you too old, don't do it. If you ain't too old, do what you feel! But don't let some idea of what people say bout age decide your life for you!"

Julia just acted shamed. "Oh! Hush, girl!"

She went home, but Clint stayed on her mind. She smiled a lot til someone interrupted asking for food or money or her time. She was soon on her way back to visit me. She is always welcome for as long as she wants. She got to know Clint a little better and went home with him one day, laughing. Clint made love to her. She was amazed . . . and young. He was in no hurry. He said, "We don't have to rush to work, rush to sleep, rush to do nothing! When we get hungry, I got a kitchen full of food and we both can cook! If you want anything, I got the money to get it! If I ain't got enough, and I blive I do, I know where I can borrow it!"

He took his time with her. They lay in bed, laughed and played with each other, talking til wee hours in the morning. He collected jazz records and put some on that went way back to when they were younger, and memory-lane pieces. He caressed her, kissed her. What she thought was old, wrinkled and ugly on her, was wonderful to him. Hell! He didn't think he was too old and she was three years younger than he was!

Her grown children were calling my house trying to run her down. They needed something. I wouldn't tell them how to reach her, just say she was out visiting. She decided to go home. Before she left he gave her a ring. A diamond ring.

She said, smiling, "Are you crazy? We too old to get engaged."

He answered, smiling, "Crazy or not, engaged or not, it make me feel awful good to still want to give a woman a diamond ring!" She smiled and hugged him. He went on, "I worked for that money! It's mine. I can do anything I want to with it! I don't care what nobody thinks! That's their business. This is mine!"

When she got home she looked so different. You see, that secret she had never felt or known about . . . she had felt it now. That Clint was a something man! It showed.

Her son was the most worried and talked to her a "heart-to-heart" talk. She told him about Clint and that she may get married. That son of hers called her "a old fool." Said that Clint was a gold digger. Clint wanted to use her! Didn't she have no sense? No shame? She was too old to think of love and way too old to think of sex . . . and shame the memory of his father! They had given her grandchildren in her old age, to fill it. Now get her senses back together and act like she had some! Many, many more things he should have been slapped out the door for. Made her feel bad and even sick, taking to her bed. Her heart hurt. The whole family was against her happiness. They knew what was best for her . . . they said. But they forgot to bring her anything to eat when they came in to get some money for a car note or a new wig.

Julia didn't know what to do. She wanted to do right, like she had always done. She got up to get something to eat and heard her son say, with his belly full of her food, "I don't care! She ain't got no business thinking of a man! She my mama!" She smiled a moment with pride at his saying, "She my mama!" Then she frowned. Hell, would he feel that way if she kept him from being happy and feeling good with his wife? She decided pride cost her too much.

That night, after calling Clint and waiting til everybody was sleep, she was packed and sneaked quietly out, got into her car and drove away . . . to Clint. She put the house up for sale in a week or so, wrote the kids what she was doing. Told them to start looking out for themselves!

Honey, them kids looked for her. Camped out in front of my house waiting for her to come by. Cussed and threatened. Said they would call the cops, have Clint arrested. Call a doctor, have Mama put away cause she was crazy.

I ask them, "Why? She ain't doing nothing to you! She done give up her whole life for you already! Now go on home and be a man and a woman and do something for your own self!"

Well, the house was sold. The money came and Julia sent her son and daughter each $10,000, saying, "That's your inheritance. The rest is mine til I die, then what's left will be yours."

Julia bought another home, not far from here, just for her. It's small. She made friends with her kids again, but told them she was renting. It had one bedroom and a half for a grandchild, sometime. Cause she was busy!

She married Clint later and for once in her life she had

someone who loved her, cared about her, made her feel good and lucky and warm and wanted, was her man.

Now, I know they was older, but evidently not too much older. They stay home a lot, they like to be alone. They make love, laugh, listen to their music, try new recipes, eat, work puzzles, or just sit in silence, together . . . at long last.

Some people would look at them and laugh! Saying, "Look at them old people!" But when I look at them I only see love. Maybe they don't make love every night, but when it's good, real good, you don't have to! Your bucket is tipped for a whole lot of reasons and making love to a person's mind and meaning it is a blessing to have . . . and to hold on to . . . forever, if you can. Don't care how old you get. I believe that from the bottom of my own happy old heart!

Having Fun

You know, you fools around in this here world and one day you done gone and got old! You starts to look back then, at all the things that done happened to you and round you, and you can see the beginning and the middle and the end of things. I think thems the times people wish they had done some things different! But . . . it's all over . . . done gone on by!

Like, a long time ago, when there was the new starting of a few families out here where I still live. My foreparents, granddaddies and grandmas and all like that, was freed from slavery, and ain't had nothing but each other and some kids they wanted to keep together and give something to for the future. Education wasn't easy to come by then, so the next best thing was land! Oh, they worked hard for them little pieces of dirt, adding to em as they could. Sweated blood and cried tears, sacrificed, went without everything to get that land! Got cheated, outtalked, overtalked, under-the-counter talked, but kept on trying! And . . . some of them made it! My family did! It was their dream, their only dream, that the land that fed and housed em, cause they built houses right out of their own lumber trees, passed right on down thru my mama and daddy and down to me and now, God willing, gon go on down to my childrens and theirs! At least down to them that don't think living in the country is for old folks and fools!

Same thing happened to our neighbors. One in particular I'm thinking of, the grandparents had worked hard, hand-hard, to get hold of 40 acres and down through the years they finally got holt of 120 acres of land! They worked that land, of course, and as their children grew up, those what didn't move away on to some city somewhere, they got married and built their own houses on that land and continued to work it. Well, after you grow up with your own trees, and the creeks you fish in are your own, you play in your own woods and catch your own rabbits and things like that, well, you love that land! And they did! They loved that land! Becomes a part of you! After all . . . it's yours!

It bears repeating, that them black people back then rooted hard, day and night, to get land and kept it up for every year they had it, to keep it! And you also know, the white men who cast their eyes on these Negroes with that good land, coveted it and sought all kinds of ways to get it! Steal it, if they could! Now, we all know it's some good white folks, but didn't none of them live round here, so the black family had to stay on guard and stay out the white folks' debt to keep that land, their land, watered heavy with their sweat! It was all they had to leave their children.

Now, they was mindful of the coming generations, since they couldn't go far back to the past. People, family, being sold and scattered in slavery, don't you see what I mean?

Now, one of them neighbors what I was talkin' about had a child born round my time, be about fifty years old now . . . like me! Name was Randy Tom! Born to the youngest daughter and raised there to young manhood. He didn't like that farm work! I think he thought he was too cute! Fact, I know he did! And since he had a uncle or two and a aunt or so what had gone on to other parts of this world, cities or towns, somewhere, he planned at his first chance to get away. I'm telling you some people don't have sense enough to see them trees, nor the creeks and things like them beautiful black-and-green fields stretching clear across the world, it seems. Growing green things just looked like too much work to Randy Tom! Me? I love all them things . . . the fresh clean air, even the cows and mules, chickens and hogs look beautiful to me! Sometimes when a person got something, they don't see it!

Well, Randy Tom got grown enough to leave that farm and went on into some service or nother. I was sorry to see him go cause I kinda liked him for myself! He was cute! But he went off and seen some of the world, and I sure know he seen plenty women cause he really loved women! Then he got out the service and got a job in one of them real big cities. A job! Working for somewhere he was never goin to be the boss! But he liked them bars and clubs where you drinks at and the fighting rings and dances, stores, and all them things that are set up for getting other people's money!

When I was growing up and wanted to stop studying and go outside to play to have some fun, my mama use to always say to me, "Any fool can have some fun! Not everybody got sense enough to put somethin in they heads to use when they gon need it later in life!" Randy Tom was having fun!

Randy Tom liked to laugh a lot and make love a lot more. Cute and handsome as he was, musta been plenty free love, but it musta not been enough cause he even paid some of them prostitutes sometime! Now, the Bible warn people bout strangers in their life and he had heard that warning from his mama just like the rest of us. But not only did he not pay it no mind, he fell in love with one of them prostitutes, a white one, and that man . . . that fool . . . married her! It's some good white women out there, but he married *her*! If she'd been Black . . . he'd still been a fool! I done seen people in love, three, four, and five times! Been in love three or four times myself! One love don't have to be the end of nothing! You hear me?!

She was probably waiting for him. Tho whatever she wanted with him, I don't know! She should have known he didn't have much sense when he married a woman who didn't even know the names of most of the men she had let into her personal body business! Oh well.

Anyway, maybe she grew to love him, cause I got to give it to her, she tried to be a good wife, she took care of him. She even gave him her hustling money til his job could sit her down! Tho I heard she couldn't hardly sell none for him coming to get her to take her home so he could have some! That Randy Tom!

When he did sit her down for good, she cooked and cleaned and became a regular wife. She never did give him no children, but maybe he never did give her none. Both wore out! I don't know! Who knows everything even bout their own business?

I do know tho, the people back here, his people, was scuffling with that property and the taxes. They was getting old and had done been tired. Most had died or been years since they heard from the ones gone away long ago, and it was hard keeping up everything. Lumber companies wanted the land, and oil companies too, and paying a lawyer them big charges to keep the mess straight that them folks kept causing us, kept our nose to the ground! Some folks lost theirs. One man got shot cause he wouldn't sell to em! Now!

Randy Tom never did bring her down here to see his family and hers didn't want to see him either! If he had brought her down here, them white folks might have killed him . . . and her too! Tho they don't usually kill their own. But it's for sure they'd a killed him! Anyway, whichever way it was, they didn't come down here! She never got to see that land he grew up on. That beautiful land bought with his ancestors' blood, sweat, and tears, laying easy in the sun. Trees swaying, full of birds. Creeks running, full of crawdads! And frogs! Woods full of fat rabbits and possums! Could catch your dinner in your backyard! Now! She probly didn't care nothing bout that kinda stuff anyway!

Anyway, the years passed. They stayed married. He had

other women, but she accepted that so there was no need for a divorce. His folks was still dying away and not too many youngsters was born to his family. Soon, when they was all dead or gone off somewhere unknown, Randy Tom inherited *all that land.* Them trees bent their heads and weeped!

He came down here . . . alone, to settle everything up. I saw him. Still cute with that swell smile! We sat out on my porch and talked. He was surprised I knew so much about him, but I reminded him people from round here are all over the world now and they writes home. I drank lemonade and he had his own gin, which he put some in my drink and we just sat there and laughed bout old times. I could tell he was restless as a flea with no dog! He went rushing back, soon as he got his business straight. Back to that smelly, crowded city where he smoked some more, drank some more, and even smoked some of that dope too! Having fun!

A few years later, Randy Tom leaped up in bed while he was making love one day. Had a heart attack! Tho how he got it I don't know cause he never did seem to worry bout nothin! Anyway . . . he died!

I ain't gonna draw this out no more cause there ain't nothin to say nohow! Cept that his white woman inherited all that land! All that dream! All that work! Yes . . . they got it back! All that land heavy with his folks' blood, sweat, and tears. Didn't cost her nothing! Randy Tom just handed it to her as he passed by on his way out of this world!

Other black people tried to buy it from her, wrote her letters and all. But she didn't answer them. Seem, after Randy Tom died, she didn't like Black folks nomore! I don't know what happened! Sometimes I pass thru that land when I go to the washing creek and it seem like them trees be bent over, all them the lumber company ain't cut down, look like they crying . . . "Where is the love?" I look at my land and I tell it out loud, "If anybody don't want to stay down here and love you,

I'll live forever for you! I'll love you!" Cause it all ended with Randy Tom. No children and no land ended the memory of his whole family! Just disappeared!

As for Randy Tom, who gave it back to them folks, I guess he had some fun. Yes, I hope he got something for his whole family's blood . . . sweat . . . and tears. Some fun. . .

The Magic Strength of Need

There's magic in every life, I do believe! You just got to find it! I don't know how to explain it, but I do know it's not the kind of magic you read about that changes everything like for Cinderella. The real magic is something you got to think on, work on! It's a job! But it's the thing that brings your life through and you have some happiness. It's a hard job cause you don't never know which way the magic is going. You got to have some kind of good sense. Common sense!

Sometime, the magic fools you! It be setting there like a big unlucky, ugly . . . unwanted something! A person will walk over it, step on it, throw it out, beat it up, hide it! Drown it in alcohol! Send it into a coma with dope! Mildew it with tears or just kick it to the side as they go out to dance! Some folks never find it!

Now, I'ma show you what I mean!

There was a girl named Burlee was born the seventh child to a big, poor family. Burlee was what is called ugly! Even very ugly! The world got a lot to pay for messing up a lotta people's minds with all that division stuff! Now, rich and poor and North and South divides things up and that's okay with things like that that can't feel nothing. But when they made ugly and pretty, they was messing with people's minds! Their lives!

I'ma tell you something! God didn't make no ugly people!

Man did! Talking about what was pretty and what was ugly. If it's somebody for everybody, then everybody is pretty to somebody! And it wasn't none of them people's business who started this ugly-pretty business to get in everybody's business like they did! You ever notice that somebody the world says is ugly, you might even agree, but when you get to know that person, you don't see ugly no more?! That goes to show you! God didn't make ugly people! Man did!

Burlee's life started off wrong cause her mama meant to name her "Berylee." A nurse who just passed right on through her life and out, looked down at Burlee and decided she had just the right look for "Burlee" and put that down. Some people are like that. Run in your life and run out, leaving you something you got to deal with the rest of your life!

Anyway, Burlee . . . was ugly. I mean ugly! Even her mama knew that. Look like Burlee knew it too, cause she looked mad right from the minute they put her in her mother's arms! Her mama said, "Hm! Hmmm! Well, things will get better." But they didn't. Burlee stayed ugly.

She was a quiet baby, just lay around looking mean. She had plenty to cry about too! Wasn't much food (well, seven kids, you know) and her diapers always wet making little sores on her baby-soft behind. She grown now and still got some of the marks! Little eyes be matted sometimes with something and nose all runny cause not enough heat for the house. They paid rent but nobody ever fixed that little house up! Paint rotted away, peeling walls, mildew even grew on the walls, and it was almost too cold for rats in there. Anyway, Burlee suffered all what being one of seven kids will make you suffer when your family is poor. The mama can try all she want too, she can't be everywhere doing everything at the same time! And sometime the dear sweet man be laying in your bed waiting for you to get through doing your work so you can come to bed and he can give you the start of something big that will wear you out some more in another nine months! He may not mean to, but, see, he may think you his magic! Thats a real funny valentine, ain't it?

However which way it was . . . Burlee was the last one cause her mama said she must be the bottom of the barrel!

Naturally, she went through the whooping cough and measles, mumps, and some of them things left little marks on Burlee's face to make that matter worse.

As she grew up, she wore all the hand-me-downs that made it down to her, went barefoot and without everything else when she had to.

As she got older, she made a secret place somewhere and would go off to that place and sit all day and think. I don't know all she was thinking of but I do know she was like a lot of people who want things. Things they see other people have. She was sick and tired and shamed of being laughed at and called "U-ga-ly!" She didn't have nothin . . . but her mama, who held her lots of times cause she knew Burlee needed it! They would talk.

"Burlee, don't cry. Don't pay no tention to what them kids say."

Burlee would cry back, "Mama, I can't help it!"

Mama would say, "You can help anything, Burlee."

Burlee would sniffle, "I try, Mama."

Mama would pet and rub. "You not ugly to me. And pretty ain't everything! Pretty is as pretty do!"

Through the warmth of her mother's love, Burlee would whisper, "What does pretty do, Mama?"

Mama would hold her closer. "Pretty go to school, study harrrrd, and learn how not to need nobody but herself!"

Burlee would smile a little. "I do that Mama. That don't make me pretty!"

Mama would smile back. "Yes it do! A little more every day! You watch and see. It adds up! You learn all you can! When you gets through learning, you gon see something!" Then another child would need Mama, cause children are jealous of each other sometimes! Mama would give Burlee a quick squeeze and turn to the next one. She was a thin, wiry woman, but she had strength she got from somewhere. She said it was from God. She had told her husband the Lord said to her, "Stop makin love" (cause she was tired). He said, "Then what I'm sposed to do?" She answered, "I don't know. You got to ask the Lord that!"

Anyway, Burlee did study hard. She was smart too! Quick to learn but always stayed in the background of things. Silent. All during high school she still went to sit in her quiet secret place, thinking. She knew what she wanted now.

Mama was bending from the weight of life . . . and was tired, very tired. When Burlee hugged her now, she would tell her, "Just hold on, Mama. I'll take care of you! I may not be getting pretty, but I am getting smart! I'm gonna find me a *rich man* and he gon marry me! I will sit you down! We'll both sit down!" Being sat down is a lotta people's dream.

Mama would smile, nod, and pat Burlee as she looked at her uncomely daughter with the shoulders and bust wider than any other part of her body. She looked like a exclamation point! Wasn't any curves and her head sat down in her shoulders with hardly no neck!

"Just be a good girl, Burlee," Mama would sigh.

"I'm too smart to be bad, Mama!" Burlee would smile and hug her one more time before some other child took over. Off she would go to her secret place to sit and dream, cause she was serious about marrying up with a Rich Man. Didn't know where they were or who they were, but they were out there! Didn't care was he black or white, just rich!

Now, it's somebody for everybody, I don't care who you are nor what you look like! At least one! Burlee had one who liked her by name of Winston. Winston wasn't too good-looking either, but he was better lookin than Burlee. The girls didn't pay him no mind. He was always leaning against some wall or tree, looking at things going on round him. He liked sports but had to work to help his mama and wasn't even in school too much, just enough to get by. He would walk home with Burlee sometime, telling her he liked her. Catching up to her he would say, "I'm going your way, Burlee." She'd fling over her shoulder, "Not far!" He'd reach for her books, she'd snatch her arm away. He'd be hurt.

"How come you don't like me, Burlee? I ain't done nothin to you! I'm always tryin to help you!" He use to fight the other kids bout callin her names. He never did low nobody to hurt her if he could help it. He got whipped hisself sometime but that never did stop him!

She would ease up. "I like you, Winston, you alright. I just ain't got no time for you!"

Reaching for crumbs again, he would say, "I know you get lonely sometime, Burlee. I even know you goes off by yourself."

Burlee would snap, "Ain't cause I'm lonely! And I told you to stop watching me! Leave me alone!"

Winston smiled. "Can't help it cause I'm lonely. I ain't got nobody, you don't go with nobody, why can't we keep company?"

Just before she ran off Burlee would snap, "Cause you too poor! I don't want nothin to do with no poor man! You just ain't rich enough!"

Winston hollered after her, "Money ain't everything! And where you gon find a rich man?!"

Which is the question Burlee thought about in her secret place that day. Which question made her come up with the idea that rich men go shopping in department stores and own em too! She was going to get a job in one and find her man! She got a part-time job fore she graduated.

She started to wearing all that makeup she got on discount to cover her pimply skin. She looked a mess! Thick pancake makeup, blue or green eye shadow, bright red lipstick and rouge, black pencil round her eyes and false eyelashes so thick and stiff with that stuff that goes on them. If she'd fallen down and hit her face it would have cracked cause it was that stiff! She looked worser . . . ugly plus ridiculous! Winston told her so and she took to hating him for it. Then her boss at the store told her if she kept wearing makeup like that, she could only clean up in the stockrooms instead of all over the store. She changed.

Now, she hung out, or rather I should say, the cleanest place in the store was round the offices where she could watch the men going in all dressed up in their suits. She was learning things too, cause she now knew the ones who owned the store were not dressed up or flashy like the ones who only worked there! After she cut down on the makeup, she decided to work more over by the beauty shop so she could maybe learn how to work on her face. Besides all the hair stuff, she saw people doing fingernails and toenails, facials and stuff like that!

Burlee didn't make much money, ain't hardly no need to say it, but she saved. From the money she insisted on giving her mama she saved 50¢ a week for four weeks to get one of them man-u-cures! The lady who gives em, a regular poor woman, thought Burlee was crazy, but took her money anyway and gave her a quick, lousy man-u-cure for her four weeks of saving and dreaming! Ain't it funny how most people, poor people, will cheat people just like themselves? And kiss the yes-yes-yes of somebody with money who wouldn't give them the time of day in return? Well, they do it all the time!

Anyway, them painted nails of Burlee's was scratched up and gone in two days! The first day she just looked at em and waved her hands in everybody's face! The second day her boss told her her work was suffering. Burlee got to work and the nails got wiped out, scratched up! Now, she didn't want to save four weeks for two days, so she decided to learn how to do it herself! That was the magic working, don't you see?! She asked the nail lady and the nail lady begrudged telling her, thinking Black folks always trying to take over things they didn't belong in. But she knew it was in the phone book, so she told her. Burlee signed up for the hand course. They didn't want her, but what the hell! Money is money!

Burlee really saved then! Her mama helped her cause she wanted her daughter to want something, to do something for herself! Sit in a chair and do white folks' nails, stead of in the kitchen or somewhere with a mop and broom! Burlee went! She practiced on her mama, which made them both happy! Little happinesses are awful good too!

Naturally, she was looking round her at school and learned about the hair. They didn't teach nothing bout no Black hair and Burlee wondered why and where she could go to learn it. There was nowhere, she was told. No school for Black hair! The magic again! Burlee talked to the only Black beautician she knew, who drank beer and smoked as she straightened and curled. She had been doing hair thirty years or so, and Burlee asked the woman to teach her. The woman thought of the competition mongst the already small clientele til Burlee said she would pay her. So, on to saving again! She learned, but she only wanted to do her own hair. She also learned she would like to own a Black hairdresser school. She talked to her mama again. Her mama offered to try to make a small loan if Burlee would pay it. She also talked to Winston, who still came around. He was working and saving his money so he could be rich someday, plus still helping his mother! That man really loved Burlee. She didn't want him from nothing!

Winston offered to give her his savings. Burlee said no to that, but would give him 25 percent of the business. That happened.

She found a small, tired-out office where a doctor used to be and rented it, getting the first three months free in exchange for cleaning, painting, and fixing it up. The landlord planned to put her out when all the work was done, so when she asked for the contract in writing, he and his wife refused! That sent Burlee to her secret place to sit and think!

When Burlee came out of that secret place, she went to the landlord and told them the bank (there was none) wanted the written agreement to give her the loan for a year's rent. Well, money and loans was part of their world so they gave her a written agreement, which Burlee put away.

She had already offered the hairdresser who had taught her, 25 percent to teach in the "Beauty College," as she now called it. You know, that hairdresser, who had long ago given up dreams and hopes except for some good man to come along, looked up at Burlee and saw a little light in her life! She accepted and took some of her little savings and got a teaching license. Before they knew it the ads was in the paper and the school was open! And doing alright!

Burlee, with 50 percent, took over the books. Winston, with 25 percent, kept it clean after leaving his regular job. Watching Burlee with his love in his eyes! The teacher, with 25 percent, taught! Plenty people came and brought their $5.00 cause it cost $8.00 at a regular shop and didn't always look any better! The students paid too, that was the main idea, so all in all Burlee was doing all right! She was saving steady and in a year or so, added a small supply shop that was 100 percent hers.

She hadn't got married yet but she was a good saver, so in a few years she bought a better home for her mama and daddy and told those sisters and brothers still at home to get out in the world and make their own way. Now!

Burlee was still looking for a rich man, but the magic was working through her!

Burlee, also, got out more and visited beauty shops and learned about that makeup stuff! Her nails were pretty all the time now, free, and she didn't have to do them herself! Pretty was still on her mind, along with that rich man. She asked one of the white ladies she met about teaching makeup at her college. The woman frowned, but Burlee said, "Just one day a week. I'll pay you good!" The woman smiled and soon was teaching. Burlee learned. Her makeup improved and the college did too. The customers were mixed colors now and she had some Latin students, so she got a Latin teacher. Just going on, chile!

Winston wanted to get married, still, but he always got the same old answer. He wasn't rich! But I'll tell you this! He was saving!!

Now, Burlee had done come in contact with all kinds of women and was always talking bout a rich man. One old one, who hustled the hard way for her living, told Burlee she couldn't get no rich man living in no house like the one she shared with her mama! Said Burlee didn't have nothing but a room! How a rich man gonna look at somebody living in a room in a house with they mama and think they deserve *him,* a rich man?! "And where your furs?" (the woman went on) "Your diamonds?" (she laughed) "And look at your clothes! Look at you! What a rich man gon see to want you for?"

Now, Burlee got mad! The magic always come when Burlee start thinking! She knew bout her clothes, but she was kinda tight with her money and, remember, she had responsibilities, her mama and all, you know! That's a long word, ain't it? Anyway, she had looked at clothes and the prices of what she liked was too high! Sides, she didn't have nowhere to go noway! She looked all over and found a lady who could sew to beat the band and wasn't doing nothing but sitting round the house getting fat. She ordered a couple outfits out of a book and paid well, but less!

Burlee also started looking round for another house, found one, a nice one, and paid down on it and was almost moving in when her father got sick. The magic worked again and she decided to stay with her mama and help her daddy and she rented the new house out. Got good rent for it! In a short time she took the basement, had Winston fix it up, and she opened a seamstress shop and school called "Fix-its." Winston got 25 percent of the business for his help. Burlee hated to give him money! Her bank accounts was getting on, chile!

She was still planning on that rich man tho. Burlee was doing all this for HIM!

Burlee's body started giving her problems round bout midnight on most nights, and all day and night on the rainy ones! She looked around her, carefully, cause she wanted to wait for her rich man, give him something special, you know? Most men want that something *special*!

I know a woman had five husbands and told everyone of them but the first one that the last one had raped her first and she had married him because she couldn't bear to be had by a man she was not married to! *And* that *he* was the first man she had ever given herself too! They *all* had loved her!

Anyway, Burlee was having these messages from her body bout some attention! Now, Winston, being in her face a lot and she trusted him, believed he loved her and thinking she could handle him, she told him he could be her lover. That magic is somethin!

She was thinking of satisfaction and he was thinking of love, so she got more out of it then he did! But, again, because he loved her, he was one happy, satisfied man! He thought Burlee and marriage were getting closer. Everything they had was already tied up!?! So!

Burlee was amazed at this feeling she felt *with* Winston but her inexperience didn't know that kind of lovemaking came with love, so she still didn't feel she felt anything *for* Winston! But a big chunk of her heart was moving over, following that big chunk of her body, into a warm, secret place inside her. The magic working again! She didn't treat him no better outside the bed tho, and she saw him only when she wanted to!

"Are you busy tonight, Mr. Winston?" She called him that in front of other people.

"What time are you thinking of, Burlee?" He just wasn't phony at all!

"I'll let you know as soon as I can, *Mr.* Winston!"

"Alright, Burlee! I blive I'm free!" He went home to get the house he had bought ready.

But one day she said, "Are you busy tonight, Mr. Winston?"

He being a little tired of her wanting, but not wanting, him, said, "Yes, Miz Burlee. Yes, I am!"

Burlee like to broke her neck when she turned it so fast she fell off that stool she was perched on! She left the college early that day and didn't even go by the other shops! Just went home and locked up in her secret place in her mind, worried! Thinking bout Winston, not wanting to. Hating him . . . she thought!

Burlee thought she would never ask him again! For the next two months or so, she didn't! Then winter came . . . and the rains. She made sure he asked her . . . and she went . . . for a while.

Thinking she was getting way off her plans for her life, she took a trip East to look over the rich men. She let a travel agency set up her schedule and she stayed at the best hotel, ate at the best places, saw theater. Always dressed . . . and always lonely. Happy, pleased, but lonely anyway. She didn't meet anyone who paid her special attention so she went home and opened up a Bar-B-Q place and served it with cloth napkins, tablecloths and real plated silver and champagne!

Everyone came! 25 percent was Winston's again and he helped her. They still made love sometime but she urged him to love someone else. He used to look down at her, when she got through moaning and groaning and hollering under him, while she told him he should find someone to love him. He thought she was crazy!

Winston became more thoughtful, giving the matter of someone else serious thought. He started taking someone he already knew out. A stash of his, I guess. The stash was a good-looking woman and she showed she liked Winston . . . a lot! She's the one who gave him birthday presents, valentine cards and Easter eggs. Cooked him breakfast sometimes, when he let her. Left pretty little notes under his pillow, if she was inside. Pretty little notes under his door, if she was outside. He wouldn't give her a key.

Burlee noticed he was pretty busy.

"Well!! I guess I lost my loving buddy?!" She smiled.

"No. You don't have to lose me!" came the reply.

"Yes I do!" she snapped back. "I don't want no disease! Who knows who else that sorry-looking woman is screwing!" She walked away.

It must have made Winston mad, cause a month or so later when Burlee said, "Are you busy this evening, Mr. Winston?" with that special light in her eyes, Winston answered, "Yes! I got a date with that beautiful woman who screws!" Then he walked away.

Couple weeks later, Burlee went to the West Coast to check on her rich man. She had plenty money now. She looked real good. She was dressed! That woman surely dressed! She moved in some fairly nice circles now and everyone knew she had that money, all them houses and business! She met her rich man! Extended her trip so they could get to know each other better, talk more. The talk finally moved to marriage cause Burlee was not going to sleep with him til it did! The commitments were almost made and he took her to his large, rambling home. The Mercedes and the Rolls in the garages. The swimming pool, the cabanas, the cook, the maid, the gardener, the thick carpets and plush luxurious furniture. Upstairs to his enormous seven-by-seven bed with the fur spread and the soft lights! Burlee was in seventh heaven! Picturing herself walking up and down these stairs, days and nights, surveying all that was hers! My, my!

She unpacked her beautiful nightgown, bought just for this occasion. Slipped as best she could between satin sheets and waited for him to come to her. A little frightened, but smiling.

Soon he came with glasses of champagne. He talked gently and softly, as he turned on the overhead lights and got into the bed and . . . grabbed her with fingers and arms that felt more like steel than flesh! He pinched and twisted the nipples of her soft human breast, then grabbed a handful of the same soft breast and squeezed hard, very hard! A thought arrived just before the small scream came. "Does he think this feels good?" He let go, so she didn't hit him, just threw her arm out, knocking over the glass of champagne she had placed on the bedside table when she was smiling. It spilled into the bed on the fine satin sheets! She was looking to see what she had done when his steel-trap hand trapped her in that warm, soft little space that is very special to us ladies. It was painful! He then pressed his hard, dry lips against hers and the hard, wet tongue through them, and proceeded to roll over on her in what I would personally call stupid jerky movements! Trying to tear the beautiful gown out the way! Did he think that was sexy? Burlee almost screamed again as it flashed through her mind all the days and nights of this there would be if she married the rich man! He was struggling around on top of her now and the only soft thing on his body wouldn't work! His face had a strange leer on it just before he raised from biting her breast, hard, and dove under the covers to sink his teeth into her leg! Burlee was confused a moment and overwhelmed by a totally new experience with what she called love! Only for a moment tho, because before even she knew it, she had thrown the cover back and slapped the living shit out of the man! Now, you can slap someone pretty hard, but to get the living shit slapped out of you . . . is to really be hit!! He screamed and grabbed his rich head that the toupee had flown off of, at the same time Burlee got up! His teeth fell from her thigh as she hit the floor and grabbed her things, rushing her exclamation point body down them beautiful stairs onto the plush carpet, where she dressed and called a cab!

The rich man came rushing down the stairs screaming, "What's the matter with you? Are you crazy?"

Burlee answered with conviction, "Nothing now! I'm alright!"

He gasped, "*You*'re alright?! Look at my face! Look at what you've done!"

As she went out the door, she said, "You look at it! I surely do not want to see it again!"

Slam! went the door!

She went straight to the airport from the hotel, waited for her plane and flew home . . . wanting *something* with all her mighty heart!

Burlee rested, had to, the first day she got home. She thought all night practically. Didn't once think of them businesses! She took herself out to dinner the next night . . . alone! She thought about the years that were passing while she fooled around with a dream that was getting raggedy!

She had plenty money! Houses! Everything but . . . *something*! She was living good, but . . . she wasn't LIVING!

Her little heart under that fine soft breast and them expensive materials, yearned and yearned.

The lobster was like cotton, tasteless. The champagne was expensive dishwater. She had ordered what she loved most but it didn't taste like nothing! She put the silver fork down and thought some more.

"What have I done with my life? What am I doing with it?" The magic was working! Her eyes filled with tears. To stop them she took a deep breath and looked around the room to see who could see she was crying. That's when she saw Winston sitting there with his good-looking girlfriend! Without knowing why, she got mad! She'd been sitting there wanting SOMETHING. Wasn't he SOMETHING?

She got up and, looking like a mad exclamation point, she pointed herself toward Winston and walked over to him and said, "I want to see you! I want to talk to you!"

Calmly Winston replied, "I'm busy now, Miz Burlee!"

Burlee looked at the woman. "No, you ain't busy! I said I want to *see* you!"

Winston stood up. "I said I was busy, so I am busy! Can't you see us sitting here?! What's wrong with you!?"

Burlee was almost crying. "You ain't busy! You ain't never

been busy when I want to talk to you, Winston! I want to talk to you, now!" She grabbed his shoulders and shook him.

He firmly grabbed her hands and removed them and, looking into her eyes, said, "If you are through eating your dinner all by yourself, go home! Go somewhere! I'm not stopping my life anymore for you to get on or get off whenever it pleases you!!"

Burlee bent her head, standing all alone, sniffling. "I got to talk to you . . . about you . . . about me. About . . . about life!"

Winston waited a few seconds, looking at her and at his girlfriend, who didn't know how to look. He said, "Go home, Burlee. I'll be by there when I am finished!"

Burlee looked at the astonished woman. "Take her home first!"

Winston sighed, "Go home, Burlee." He walked her to her car. She grabbed him and pleaded. "Come now! Pleasssssse come now!" (We all know how that is.)

Winston remained silent, looking at her. "What did you find out there in the West that got you so ready for me?"

Burlee screamed at him, "Do you still love me?"

Winston opened her car door. "Get in, go home. I'll be there soon."

She got in, but as he walked back to the club she screamed, "You promised you would love me forever! Don't you lie to me!"

He turned. "I didn't say I'd *wait* forever tho!"

"Forever ain't over!" she screamed!

"No, you told me to find somebody else!" he threw back.

She looked tired. "I didn't know I was lyin. Oh hell! Winston, can't you see I love you . . . now. I want you to love me . . . now."

He looked at her for a long time, turning his head to the side. She looked up at him, feeling the very air against her perspiring, hot skin, felt the very sweat in her armpits, the very real need in her soul.

He smiled. "I'll be over in a little while."

She left thinking, "He's almost rich!"

Later, he did go by. Yes, they talked a long time. Yes, he still loved her. Seems some people is just for some people! Yes, he made love to her, the kind she understood. Yes, they soon got married.

Burlee lately gave Winston a little son and named it Winston Burl. I'm glad they got that over with and out the way before they had a daughter!

I see her sometimes. She is happy. Winston takes care more of the business cause she takes care more of the house. She wants to! Says she done worked enough in her life for three people. Says all these white women tryin to get out in the workplace, don't understand that that's where her people been all the time! Say she tryin to get out of it! She still takes care the money and the books tho! She also got her pet projects. She holds free classes every week for poor young girls and boys she gets from schools, to teach them how not to feel left out of life. Burlee always looks carefully over them youngsters for the ones the world might call "Ugly." She asks them to do *her* a favor, and sends them through all her beauty stuff for a week, free. So they will know how to do something for themselves to make themself feel better! When they smile at their new selves in a mirror, Burlee laughs a deep, happy laugh and sends them on their new way.

There is magic in life, if you can find it. It's a job tho! Oh yes, you got to think . . . and work on it! And don't forget love . . . there is magic in love too! Work on it!

Swingers and Squares

Ain't life funny? This life thing will drive you crazy if you let it! Me? I'm a hundred-degree woman and I ain't goin to let it! But life is funny, and some people don't know how to live it! They fools! They just come here and breathe and go thru the motions, as they say, then get on way from here! Ain't done nothing! Ain't lived! They just squares! I know, cause I got a window to one right here, next door, my neighbor. Not like me! I meant to do my livin and I have!

Now, like love. Oh, how sweet love is! I love love . . . all kinds of love! Any love, anytime, anyplace, chile! See? You got to taste of life! That what the books say. That's what I done and I ain't sorry one bit!

Take my friend next door. She been married to the same man twenty or twenty-five years! I don't know exactly cause I been busy living and ain't had time to know *all* her business. But I do know I ain't never ever seen her in a bar or no places to meet nobody else! Sho ain't gon' meet nobody else in church with that man sitting up side of her!

I remember when we was all younger and just getting married and all. Her husband was nice-looking. They made a nice-looking couple . . . got to give em that! But, honey, me and my husband, we was good-looking! My husband was fine, fine, fine. Didn't turn out to be worth nothing, but he sure was fine! Tall, big shoulders, football player–looking shoulders! Head full of hair and a smile to break your heart for days! He wore a big rhinestone ring trying to be a diamond, and cufflinks to match. Tried to smoke cigars. Wore them pointy-toe shoes. Oh, he was sharp! A heartbreaker! And that's what he did . . . broke my heart! Ten months we was together. That's all! Them women wouldn't leave him alone! I tried to keep up with him, going to all them parties and nightclubs and hanging round the pool hall, but I couldn't! I had one baby and one on the way when he left! Ohhh, I missed him! He had a way of slapping your hips when he made love. Hurt . . . but I loved it! Been looking for it, just never found it again. Yeah, I tried to keep him, but he didn't have good sense enough to try to keep a good woman like me, giving him a family! He never did nothing for me or his kids after that, cept once in a *big* while! He still round here! I know where he is. Right up there on that hill, done married a widow woman had a house! He got a real diamond now!

When I got home with my second baby from the county hospital, Lana, that's my neighbor, was just getting home with her first. He must didn't never make love to her if it took two years to have one child! I remember he carried her up the steps. Ain't that silly?! Her mama was carrying the baby and he was carrying her! Ain't that cute? Shit! Two years later they had another baby. And so did I! Me, three. Them, two. She said they planned theirs. Mine was a accident. Right in the middle of my good times! Chile, I was having a ball!

I had a little ole tiny job at the Hoot Owl niteclub and the lady next door watched my kids til they went to sleep. When I would get in in the morning I'd be so tired, but I'd fix them some toast and fall into bed and sleep while they play. See, the important thing is somebody in the house with em. That ole grown-ass daughter of mine messed it up once by burning herself half up when I was sleep! I'd been drinking and it was hard to wake me up. Well, I hafta drink doing the kind of job I do, keeping customers happy! Anyway, she made me so mad! Then she had to go running over to Lana's, and Lana put the fire out and even took her to the doctor's when she couldn't wake me up! Wasn't even my doctor! Cost me $30! I still owe it! I tole her to stay out of my business! Then I gave my daughter a good whipping for playing with fire and ruining my sleep! Hell! I had to go back to work, didn't I? I was sure glad when they got big enough to take care of themselves and the new baby!

Lana was always so silly! Didn't have a big thought in her head! Now, she sent her children to dancing school and them poor kids had to go take piano music lessons three times a week. And do you think she even let them be free after that? No, chile! Even in the summertime they had to come in the house by 6:30, light outside or not! My daughter told me! See, you got to have some sense and trust your kids. I trust my kids. They could stay out and play till 10:00 or 11:00, cause I remember how much fun I use to have playing! I didn't mess up my kids' fun! You got to remember when you was a child, when you get to be a parent! Sides, I had to work! I had to trust em!

Then when all the kids got measles and whooping cough and all them things? Lana practicly kept a doctor at her house. All that money! Me, I rubbed baking soda and water on my kids and taught them how to do each other. They came out all right . . . just a few marks on they faces and backs and arms. But look at the money I saved! Didn't have it anyway! You got to dress when you work at a niteclub! Besides, I had a problem cause my son had started taken my clothes to sell to get sweets and things to eat! He wasn't never no good! Just like his daddy! Waiting till I leave, then be taken my clothes! Well, you do the best you can as a mother, but it don't do you no good! They don't preciate it!

Well, the years passed and that Lana hadn't progressed or changed one bit. Still doing the same ole things! Only difference was she was staying home now, not working. Just staying home fixing lunch for them kids and making them come home from school, walk three blocks, to eat lunch! Said they needed something hot when I told her she could be restin. Told you she was dumb! Kids can take a lot, and don't need a lot! Some folks just ain't got no sense!

I could tell what time it was, if I was home, by the time they turned their lights off! At 10:00 at night all the lights go out except the bathroom light they always leave on. She didn't never go nowhere! I know cause one of my daughters practicly lived there. She wouldn't let her daughter spend the night over here tho! That ole bitch! Just cause I had a man over here for the night sometime! Scared her chile gon learn somethin new! Ain't I human? She probably needed to learn somethin new sides all that boring stuff she had over there at home. Jive-time stuff!

Do you know, when them kids got to be teenagers, her kids was still wearing all them starched, stiff dresses? All that work? I'm telling you that woman Lana was a fool! Now, I got good sense as anybody and I know kids don't pay no mind to what they wearing! I let mine go down there to the secondhand store and pick out what they wanted. That's what being a kid is all about! Learning to choose stuff, do something different! Doing things for themself! I couldn't work that hard round the house no more. I had had bout fifteen miscarriage, well, that's what I called em! And since I still had to work at the bar, I needed my strength for better, more important things than standing up over no ironing board doing dresses and things. Let em learn how to do their own, anyway! That's how they get to know bout life!

My son started staying out nights bout then. Well, boys will be boys! I don't want no sissy! He sposed to be a man someday! One day when I was laying out in the backyard sunning and having a cold beer with a friend and was talking bout having the landlord clean up this yard cause it was a mess, Lana called to me over the fence. I was so comfortable, but I got up and went to see what she wanted. She told me her husband saw my son hanging over there by the pool hall everyday when he should be in school, and sometimes very late at night when he should be in bed! Now, her husband works for the gas company and gets around quite a bit. I told her to mind her own business and tell her husband to mind his too! I'll run my family! Just run her own! Made me mad! In front of my company! My son wasn't gon be nothing but like his daddy, noway! I knew he was gonna have womens taken care of him someday. Wasn't he already using me? I tole him . . . "make em pay!" I don't want him laying on me all his life! He sure was goodlookin enough. Lana was just jealous cause she didn't have no son! Uh-huh! I had somethin she didn't have!

Bout that time Lana's husband got down real sick . . . some accident on the job, I think. He had to stay home in the bed. That Lana went on out and got a job! A job! I said to myself, "Good! Let's see how you make it out here stead of hiding in them four walls, you so smart! Thought you'd buy a house, huh? Now, let's see you pay them notes!"

Well, she worked while he just layed around the house! I said to myself again, "I bet them kids don't come home for lunch no more!" But they did! And I thought them starched white blouses and things would go too, but they didn't! The oldest girl and her daddy did it! Slaves! She was raisen a slave! And makin a woman outa her man! Ain't life funny?

Time passed and everything got back to normal, I guess.

Then the school cital or recital, whatever it was, it came up. My daughter, who hangs over to Lana's house all the time, worried me to death to go. Finally my boyfriend, at that time, told me to go, so I did. Honey, you could have blown me away when I looked up on that stage and saw my daughter singing! Alone! She wasn't singing nothing I liked or even knew, but she was singing pretty! "Look what I have done," I thought. I was so proud! One of Lana's daughters played the piano and the other played the violin with her singing. They played through the whole show, with her and everybody else! I got tired of them. They was alright but nothing special. Lana and her husband were there, of course, just grinning at the stage like fools! When the show was over and them kids ran to them, they grabbed them and said, "These are my daughters!" and the daughters said, "This is my mama! This is my daddy!" My daughter ran to them too, til I waved at her, then she came over to where I was. She didn't holler out that I was her mama, but she ask me to meet her teachers. I looked around me and pulled on out of there. I told her, "Honey, I done told them teachers so many lies, I don't want them to see me!" I laughed and thought she would, but she didn't! Too much hanging round Lana's house! She was losing her sense of humor! I told everybody at the bar about her later, but they didn't believe me!

High School graduation time came and, of course, my daughter needed a dress . . . a white one! She liked to drove me crazy! See, my nerves is bad! I mean it! I told her I had a red dress she could wear, pretty dress, off the shoulders and all! She didn't want that. She cried and flung herself all over the house! I had to leave there to get some peace sometime! Just go on and go to work early, that's what I'd do. I knew my other, younger daughter was stealing, and I was wishing she would steal one for her sister to wear to graduation. But that fool never caught on and a person can't *tell* her daughter to steal! Hell, least not me, I ain't that kind of mama!

Lana, finally, said she would make one for her to graduate in if *we* bought the material! Ain't that something! If you gon do something, do it all! Do it right! Have some class bout yourself! Ain't life funny? Some people just don't know from nothing, and she was always acting like she knew everything! Anyway, we got the material some kind of way, and Lana made the dress. I didn't get to go to the graduation tho, I had a awful hangover and couldn't move my head. See, I'm not well. I been through a lot . . . all by myself! Lana done had help—a husband. My daughter was beautiful tho, they told me bout it!

Problems never end, honey! My daughter wanted to go to college! Seems Lana's daughter was going. I told my child she better wake up and see what's happnin! College ain't nothing! I could help her get a job at the club where I work, but I never could be able to send her to no college! It wasn't gon help her no way! She had already done more than anybody in our family had ever done when she graduated from high school! Hell!

She settled down and pouted around the house for a month or so. Wouldn't take that job at the club! It all ended up with her marrying up with a soldier and she lived in Germany. I heard from her sometime. She divorced, but still lived and worked over there. Won't come home! She didn't get no babies. She smart, that one! My other daughter had three! Dropped out of school, married some jive-time boy, just like her daddy! Ain't life funny? No matter what I do I can't get they daddy out of them! That's what cause all their troubles! My son went to prison.

Well, time goes on by.

My oldest daughter never has come back home and she comes over here to New York sometimes. She's married again, some half-rich, educated man she met in Italy. I think that's where she lives now. She got two children now I've never seen! They don't know they grandmama! A child should know the grandmama! My daughter don't send me no money either! Never! And I'm her mama . . . raised her! And she know I need it! I wrote her and told her bout my troubles. Back gone out . . . knees all swollen from arthritis and all! All these things I got working to support my kids! Being a mother! That Lana turned my baby against me, that's what! I shoulda kept her away from over there!

My other daughter got five kids now and she always trying to leave em here with me! I say, "Uh-uh, uh-uh! No, you don't! I raised mine, now you raise yours!" She be drunk and she try to fight me sometime! She living with her fifth man! I tell her, "Fight him!" I have to call the police sometime! No matter how you raise them, they ain't gon come out right if it ain't in em! My son was out for a while from that prison, but he back in again now. When he was out, he got drunk and came over here and tried to get in bed with me! Said everyone else had! The liar! If my boyfriend, at that time, hadn't come in, I'd a had to fight my own son! As it was, he left, telling my friend not to "fall in, cause you'll never find your way out like I did!" Ain't that terrible? Do everything you can and still . . . Ain't life funny?

I know you want to know, so I'll tell you! Lana's daughters. One lives in New York. Done married up with somebody big and travels a lot. She in concerts and things. The other one teaches in some college, married to some professor! Ain't done nothing but marry and settle down to slavery just like their mama! That's what you go to college for? To get married?! That's phoney! Me, I ain't no phoney! I'm for real!

Lana? I still think she stupid sometime. Her husband went back to work and worked til he retired. Ain't never done nothing big! Them two people still over there, next door, after all these years! I don't care if they did fix it up and added rooms to it and all. They put up a big fence between us on accounta my landlord never did clean up that yard! It's a mess! They take trips and all that square stuff and keep their grandchildren. Four, I believe. They repeating all the things they already done. Starched dresses and shirts and hot lunches! And smiling about it! Ain't life funny?

It's some people in this world never do learn! I rather be a swinger any day than be one of them squares! They fools and don't know it! Ain't life funny?

I got to rest now . . . I hurt!

Down That Lonesome Road

First off, let me let you know, I am not a gossip! Can't stand em! I'm known for that! I don't tell nobody's business . . . and I know everybody's! Now, that ain't hard to do out here, living somewhere a long way from everywhere. Nothing but sky, trees, and lotsa land stretching out to all over. With people living bout a seven- or eight-minute walk to the next place, and we mostly walkin, ain't too much visitin. So you see, it can get mighty lonesome if you ain't got your company at home with you!

Next off, I'm the type of person who likes to see other people be happy! I'm known for that too! Don't like no misery round me. If I let myself I'd stay busy, wouldn't never get no rest. But I don't let people run over me with their needs, cause I got a family of my own. Me and my husband been married plenty years, so he don't require much no more. But I gives him a lot cause he a good man, and from all I see and hear in this here world they is hard to come by, and since I'm pass the age to keep coming by men, I take care the one I got! He a little plump, hair almost gone on top, but so am I plump. I got my hair tho, lots of it! I also got four kids. Raised well, grown and gone. I don't blive kids should stay at home after they grown less they sick or need some of my lovin. So they welcome to visit or stay awhile, but they know they got to go. I'm known for that!

My favorite hobby is collecting things. Josh, my husband, say it's junk. But you be surprised how many things you or somebody might need some day. I got almost everything! My basement is full, honey, to the top! Round here when people need something old, they say, "I bet Bertha got one!" And usually I do, or know where they can find it. My husband say long as it ain't all over the yard, okay. I make my extra money like that. I'm known for that. They talk to me too, bout their lives and how they feel sometime.

One thing I notice the most about people is the loneliness. Oh, there's all kinds of loneliness. And in this far-off place, well . . .

We got trees everywhere all over the place. All kinds of trees. Tall pines, cedars, huge weeping willows, large, large magnolias, all that. Now, you may not know why I'm saying this, but them trees surrounds everybody's place, and when the moon comes up . . . Lord, Lord. You remember that ole song, "Don't the moon look lonesome shining through the trees?" Well, I can tell you, that's the sad truth. You needs you somebody out here in these great big black nights shining with that fat ole moon. Or a real good friend like me to talk to. I'm known for that! Cause I blive in keeping other people's secrets and mostly do. But I'm going to tell this one. Cause it's a real good thing bout how funny life can be and how one human being really do need another one!

I got a friend, Oraliza, almost my best friend. My husband is my best friend, see! I call her Ora sometime. I don't know how old she is, ain't never asked her cause that's her and the Social Security office business. She ain't old tho, bout thirty-five or forty. Her husband died bout a year ago. I don't know bout all how their lives was but they was company and they was good to each other. They worked hard for and with each other on their land and house. That's love to me! Cause don't too many people like to do no working.

Anyway, he had something ate his life away . . . and

he died. He was much older than her when they married and they was married bout twenty years. He come sick 'bout three years fore he died. They musta had a savings cause she never came over here to borrow nothing! I mean money, cause it's too far to walk for a cup of sugar or something like that! She mourned when he died, naturally, but she kept on going cause what you gonna do if you still breathing? Just keep on, that's all!

Ora was nice-looking, not too fat, just pleasingly plump. A little gray in her hair. She wasn't nothing to shout about like no Mae West or nothing, but she was sweet and loyal, kind and soft-spoken. Kinda shy too. She didn't usually have no one-track mind, but sometimes your mind can get on a track and you can't do nothing with it!

One day, when this all started, she came through the early-morning mist, trees still reaching up to heaven looking like they praying, you know? I said to myself, "Lord, I don't want no company this early in the morning!" But I pulled that ole indoor-lookin robe round me and put the coffee on. I knew her husband's death had done come down on her and she needed a friend. My turn might come, anytime, so I was glad she had come to me cause I might have to come to her someday. Lord forbid it! Friends is friends, whether they ready or not!

Well, she surprised me! Oh, she missed her man, she had loved him, but she wanted to talk about sex! Sex!

Seems, naturally, she was a warm woman and her husband had been sick three years and gone one and she hadn't made love in all that time . . . naturally. Now, don't think she was no sex maniac or nothing . . . or . . . that any other woman who thinks about sex is. Normal is normal and human is human. She said, some nights, whether she want to think about it or not, the thoughts come. Just come, that's all! No love in four years! Well, me, I gets sick of it sometime. Only sometime. But that's cause my man is right beside me! Every night!

Sometime I think I want to be alone and quiet, but if he was dead and gone, maybe I wouldn't want to be alone and quiet . . . I'd want him. She didn't wear the subject out, but it was clear to me cause my understanding is big.

There were some single men around, mostly too young. And they was looking for someone their own age . . . pretty and ready to trot! They didn't know these older ones still trotting too! They only learn that when they get older! The other single men was mostly old and alone cause they too mean and evil to get along with. Now, I had a cousin, back from the wars, who lived in a little house over cross and down the road. He was the right age but he had a leg missing and a big scar cross his back. He was so shamed of em he just never hardly came out. Had done stepped on some bomb or something and left things important to him in some country he hadn't never even planned on going to, while them people who did have something to protect in that country sat up somewhere counting they money and drinking fancy liquor. They didn't even know his name and he almost died for them! We called him "Boxer."

Anyway, all the single women who might need a man, didn't pay him no mind. None! So he just worked his little land and fixed little broken-down things for other people and doing odd jobs. Kept to himself. But we know . . . he saw that moon shining through the trees too. I thought he had two minuses . . . no leg and no confidence, no more.

Ora hired men to do her little plowing and stuff, but she had never hardly thought of Boxer, cause of his leg. She thought he was a cripple or something. But he wasn't no cripple. He just didn't have one leg.

Anyway, to get back to Ora on that morning, she had a sister who was telling her to come visit her in the city and she was going. She wanted me to look after her place till she got back. I was glad to, glad she was going somewhere where she might meet somebody nice. You know what I mean? A future husband . . . or maybe just a load off her mind! She left, dolled up and smiling, that truck bouncing all the way down that lonesome road to the city.

Ora came back, early in the morning again, to tell me about her trip. About the time she had. I just knew she had met somebody . . . had a nice time and all. Even nice women got sense enough to know when to have a nice time. You won't blive this but this is what she told me.

She did have a nice time, meeting relatives, eating a lot of good food, talking bout old times, things like that. Then she was silent for a minute, looking out the window. My eyes started to droop as I thought of my warm spot in the bed under my husband's warm back. Then she said when her sister use to go to work everyday, she would get on a bus and ride all around to see the city. Walk a lot and stuff like that. Then one day as she was getting near the time to come home, she was walking and decided to buy some books to bring back. She turned into a store that didn't have any books in the window, but said Bay Books on the outside. She went in and there was hundreds of magazines and books with lots of people standing round reading them. When she turned to the counter to ask about some good novel books like *Come by Here* and *Gone with the Wind* or something, she saw rows and rows of funny-looking things standing up. When she looked closer she saw they was private parts! Men's private parts! Pink ones, white ones, yellow, gray, red, black, and brown ones! All sizes! She said she liked to died! She turned and ran out the store, seeing that all the people standing in there was men. She caught the first bus passing and went home! My eyes was wide open now. I'm known for being alert!

She went on talking, telling me she lay in bed that night just thinking about it. By morning she had decided to go back, but since she was shamed, she didn't want to go in as herself so she needed some disguise. The next day after her sister was gone to work she did it. She took her false teeth out, took a eyebrow pencil and made moles and warts and deep wrinkles. Even blacking the two front teeth she had left, with the pencil. Tied a kerchief round her head, dressing poorly. Now, I'll tell you, didn't nobody know her in that city noway! She coulda just walked in that store without a backward glance. Still, she did all that, then got on a bus and rode to the store. Rode so long she got scared she had passed it and almost cried, but finally saw the landmarks (country people make those) and got off the bus.

It was raining, the sky was dark. So when she went in the store it was kinda empty, from the rain, I guess. She was so glad! She stood there and looked at those rows and rows of men's parts. Finally she mumbled to the man clerk that she wanted one. He showed her round all the different types and colors. She kept watching the door cause she was shamed to be there and didn't want no men coming in seeing her, a woman, there. He showed her more, all round corners and things! More! Can you magin?! I ain't never, never even *heard* of such a things! She said there was all sizes! He asked her what size she wanted! How did she know?! Now, country people mostly want the most for their money, so as to get the most for her money she picked a bargain, she picked the biggest one. You know? He said no, that was for display, that she should pick a smaller one for herself. She said she looked very stern and said, "It's not for me!" He said, smiling, "Of course not!" She picked a smaller one, then he asked, "Vibration?" She said, "Vi-what?" He repeated it as two men came in. She cringed. "No! No! No vi . . . Just give me that one! How much?" He said, "What color?" She said she almost screamed, "I don't care what color . . . just give me one!" He laughed and she cringed again. He put it in a bag and rang the register as she paid him. Someone new came in the door. She cringed again and screamed, "Give it to me! Let me get out of this—this sex den!" She snatched the bag and rushed out mumbling "Dirty men!" with her package gripped tightly in her little sweaty hands. She said she ran around the corner not scared, but shamed. Shamed! That poor child. But I'da been shamed too. Not to buy it! But to let other people, specially men, know I needed it! On the other hand tho, ain't it normal to need lovin? Made me think! I better get ready cause my husband's old and he been working hard all his life. He may go first and I may not be through. Then I got a little mad cause we have to be shamed bout this human stuff. Don't we meet each other on the path of life? Don't that tell us we all human? Why talk about each other? If I thought you'd ever meet Ora I wouldn't tell you this business of hers. And if you ever do meet her, you better not say nothing! Don't even open your mouth!

Anyway, she say when she got home and unpacked . . . there it was! She put it in the drawer then changed it to the closet. Later she put it in the icebox. Scared and shamed less somebody accidently come upon it! She laughed a sad little laugh when she said, "It don't fit noway. It was too big a bargain!"

I shook my head. "My, my. All that trouble for nothing."

She smoothed her hair in exasperation. "Now I got it, I don't know what to do with it!"

I thought of my basement. "Well . . ."

But she went on, "I can't throw it away. When I did that, my damn dog found it in the woods and brought it back."

I gasped, "Jesus, Mary, and Joseph!"

She sighed. "I ran in the house and put that thing in a flowerpot and covered it with dirt."

I nodded my approval. "Well, nobody sure ain't gonna be lookin in no dirt in a flowerpot."

She shook her head. "No . . . but it be just my luck for the damn thing to take roots and grow, then I have a parts plant!" We laughed like little girls.

I thought a minute, of my basement again. "Well . . ."

But she said, "I would burn it but the thing is thick rubber or plastic or something. It would stink and it would take too long! Smokin up my whole yard! Lord, I don't know what to do with the thing!"

I told her to hide it in the barn till I come over. I want to see something like that, that you can just put in your pocket and carry round with you! And that would give me time to think.

She said, "My helper goes in that barn. I'll find somewhere. Maybe the chicken house, cause I always gather the eggs." That was settled.

Bad as I wanted to, I didn't get over there for a month or so. My cousin, Boxer with one leg, got sick and I had to haul food over there and clean him up and the house. We even worked his little land for him. I blive he tried to kill himself by taking too many of his pills. I was thinking of Ora and him when I went by there accidently and found him and called the doctor. We saved him. He wasn't too happy with me about it tho. Just sighed a lot and wouldn't talk much. Just lay there looking at the moon coming up through the trees. Then in the dawn, watching the sun come up on another day.

I had to also feed all them animals and things Boxer found and kept. He took up a lot of time caring for birds with broke wings or legs, even chickens with broke legs or hurts, rabbits or kittens, dogs, whatever is sick or hurtin . . . he heals em. Builds them a nice warm place to heal in. Once, and this is the truth, he stepped on a snail a little and cracked its shell. He felt so bad he went and found a good empty shell, put corn meal in it, and attached them till the poor little snail moved from his broken home to his good one! I admire that. Most people kick things out the way . . . or kill em!

I watched him. A fine-lookin grown man. A nice man who didn't have no woman to love him. To watch that fat, lonesome moon with. To stay in from the rain with. My mind just accidently thought of Oraliza.

Boxer was much better and I was planning to go over to

Ora's to see that thing and see what I could get started. I'm known for getting things started. But she came to my house first, to tell me she was going back to the city. Her sister had written she had someone who wanted to meet her. She was bright and smiling and eager to go!

She hit me on my back. "Girl, maybe this is it! I may not have to grow old alone after all. I sure been praying in that church . . . this might be the answer!"

I smiled. "Honey, don't I wish it for you!" And I meant that, Boxer or not! Still I said, "But I ain't feeling so good and can't run over to check on things for you."

Her eyes opened wide in alarm.

I said, "I'm going to send my cousin, Boxer, over to look out for you. He a man and knows more to look for than I do."

She breathed relief. "Oh, Boxer. Is he still round here? I never see him at church or nowhere."

I worked on. "Yeah, he's still here and a good man too! A working man! Knows how to do a lotta things. You oughta hire him when you need a man helper. He do a whole lot more then some of them what takes advantage of you cause you a woman!"

She was too excited to think about work. "Really? Ain't he lost a leg . . . or a arm or something?"

I caught her up gently. "He ain't lost his mind. It was his leg . . . and he got another one just like it! He still got everything else he need." But she didn't get my meaning.

She said, "People like that gives me the creeps . . . pieces missing from their body."

I got a little mad. "He don't give me the creeps, but I ain't you. Another thing, it didn't give you no creeps looking at that thing you got with no man at all 'tached to it!" Then I softened cause she didn't mean no harm. "Where is that thing anyway?"

"Oh!" She remembered. "It's still buried in the chicken coop. Everytime I get eggs, I think of it and wish I hadn't been lookin for a bargain." She looked off cross the fields. "But maybe if this man turns out right, I'll have somebody in my life again."

I smiled. "Well, get on outa here and go see!"

She turned to leave. "Alright then, Bertha. See if Boxer will look out for me and I will pay him." She left, going down that lonesome road again.

I told Boxer and he agreed, reluctantlike. He knew her but I don't think he lowed hisself to think too much on no woman. Was shamed of that leg and didn't have no confidence.

Oraliza got back quicker than I expected, her face all long and sad and everything. I asked, "You didn't like him?"

She sniffed. "Chile, that man thought I had some money with a sprawling country home! I don't know what was wrong with my sister!"

I said, "Mercy!"

She sniffed on. "He want to take me to a hotel the first night! He couldn't hardly remember my name!"

I said, "Have mercy!"

She coughed, sniffed, sighed. "You know I needed to, and I wanted to, too. But it was just plain ole sex. I wanted to be loooved." Her arms was on the table. She laid her head down on em then raised up again, sighing heavy. "I wanted to meet somebody what was gonna want a life with me."

I moved round in my seat, uncomfortable cause she was hurtin, "Well, Ora . . . that man didn't know you enough to marry you!"

She smiled sadly. "I know that . . . but he didn't even try to."

I didn't know how to say it, but I said anyway, "Well, why didn't you least let him love you some and give your mind some relief? I mean . . . a little wouldn't hurt . . . would it?"

She sniffed and lay her head down again. "I did." I almost smiled for her, but she went on talking and stopped me. "It was like he was making love to a hole in the mattress! Pounding . . . like I was the ground and he was running a race on me! Wasn't no feeling . . . no lovin feeling. He made me feel like a . . . a . . . tennis ball, batted from one side to the other!" She was talking so softly I could hardly hear her. But I knew what she meant cause I wasn't born this morning! She went on talking mostly to herself.

"I was thinking too, did he have a disease? Was he clean? How I know what he does? Who he is? I told God, 'Please don't look. I'll never do this again.' And I won't!"

"Be careful!" I told her, "cause you don't never know bout life and what you'll end up doing!"

She looked at me, her eyes full of her little heart and so sad. "Bertha, I ain't gonna keep coming over here bothering you with my problems. You been a good friend and . . . I'm gonna get better."

I reached out to pat her shoulder. "I know that, Ora, that's what a friend is for, when you need em, and don't you think I don't know how important what you talkin bout is."

She looked into her cup of coffee I had poured a little homemade brandy in, took a big swallow and looked out the window, but she wasn't seeing nothing. "Every morning when I wake up, no matter how good I feel . . . I feel bad. Empty. Alone. Last thing at night when I go to bed . . . it's the same thing. The next day? It's the same thing all over again. I'm lonesome. Ain't nothing changing in my life. Everyday . . . everyday . . . it's the same. I don't want a life like this . . . I'm used to somebody."

I thought of her old husband and it's like she read my mind. She said, "I ain't used to no rip-roaring sex life . . . but I am used to my man." I thought of my own old man and I understood. She went on, "Life is meant to be loved while you're young."

I said, "While you're old too!"

She sniffed again. "Time is going by so fast, even if it does drag every day. My life is passing away. Oh, Bertha, am I going to live and grow old and die . . . all by myself from now on?"

I started to say something but poured me a drink instead. I wasn't gonna lie to this woman. I didn't know no answer.

We both wiped a few tears from our eyes. Yeah, I cried too! I'm softhearted. I'm known for that. Wasn't no tears in her voice tho.

"I got some love I want to share! There ain't nothing . . . sweet . . . in my life anymore. All day, every day, all night, every night, all the same . . . just me." She looked at me. "Oh, not just sex, not just sex, Bertha."

Now, you may think she was overdoing being alone. But you just wait . . . and hope you ain't never that alone in some place like out here in the nowhere land—or anywhere else! She only had three or four years of this bad luck, but who are we to judge what is a hurry or not? Or too much? Or too little? We ain't no judge, that's what!

I cut her off. "I know what you mean! You don't think I love that ole fat-bellied, bald-headed man of mine cause he's a sex king, do you?"

We laughed a little, drank a little more, and soon she left, walking slowly, all dejected . . . out the yard, going down the road . . . to her empty house.

I thought about her off and on through the night. When I went to bed, I rubbed my old man's bald head and kissed his double chin, loving him. He just grinned and hugged me. The next morning, over my coffee, I tried to think of something to help my friend. Weeelll . . . I thought of Boxer. I wanted to help both of them.

Now, the way my thoughts went is this. They both had two minuses. One, no confidence, two, shame, of how one looks and the other feels. See? Now, if you take one minus and cross it over another one, you get a +. Then, if you can get the other minus on top of the other one, you get a =. Then, 1 + 1 could = 2! See? My problem was to get them last 2 minuses on top of each other to get to that = equal stuff.

So . . . I lied. Well, I had to do something!

The next time Boxer came by I asked him, "Say, Boxer, what you been saying to Ora when you over there working?"

He looked at me wondering what I could be talking about. "Nothing."

I smiled just the right amount of serious. "Well, you must be saying something, or doing something. That woman say three nights since she been home she been dreaming sexy dreams about you!"

He looked at me like I was crazy, but I could tell it pleased him. "Dreaming? Sexy? Of me? You lyin!"

I helt on my act. "Yes, you! You musta put something on her mind."

He scratched his stomach, slowly. "What kind of dreams, you say?"

I had better sense than to lie too much. "I can't tell you that!" I grinned. "She would die if she knew I told you. When you go over there to work this morning, don't you tell her I told you! I mean that!"

He shook his head in bewilderment. "I don't . . ."

I pushed him toward the door. "Go on over there now and work like you sposed to. And try to do a few little extra things, cause she need help. Put up a shelf or something. Womens always need something done in the kitchen. She ain't had no man to help her in the house for most four years! Go on! Do what I tell you!"

He ain't crazy either. "Bertha, what you tryin to do? That woman don't want no one-leg man hobbling round in her house . . . or in her face!"

I got mad or exasperated. "If you ain't nothin but that leg you done had to leave somewhere, then I guess you right! But I didn't say do nothin cept what any man would do for a woman is alone and may need something done . . . round her house. You fixes things, don't you?"

He was leaving, waving his hand back out at me. He limped a little cause he took that extra leg off whenever he was home. He limped to his truck and got in, setting there a few minutes, then he drove off, slow and thoughtfullike. Down that same lonesome road . . . to Oraliza's house.

Now see, I know, when you tell somebody somebody likes them, they may not believe you, but they tends to pay more tention to that other somebody. Watches them. In other words, it puts somebody on somebody's mind, whether they thought they liked them back or not! *And* if a person is a nice person, while they being watched, it's gonna show and they might really end up liking that person they wasn't even thinking about in the first place! I know what I'm talkin bout, even if you don't!

The next time I saw Ora, and I made sure it was soon, I took her a jug of homemade wine and told her, "Drink a little of this every day. I hear there's a fever virus going round and we sure don't need to catch it. This will help keep it away, least it always has for me!"

She took it, frowning. "Really? I sure will take some, cause I can't afford to get sick. Thank you."

I asked, "How you doing? Garden alright?"

She smiled. "Yes, that Boxer sure is a good worker."

I smiled. "He sure must like you!"

She frowned. "Why you say that?"

I kept smiling. "Cause he told me he didn't know why, but he been dreaming of you almost every night since you been back home." I whispered, "Sexy dreams, chile!"

She looked surprised. "What?"

I waved my hand at her. "Well, don't look at me! It must don't mean nothing. He ain't said nothing to you, has he?"

"No!" came the quick reply.

I said, "It must don't mean nothing then. Just something he told me. I'm his cousin, you know, we always did talk. Give me a glass of water so I can go." We went in the kitchen and one of the walls was covered with new shelves! I said, "My, they sure look nice!"

She smiled and looked at em. "Yes. Boxer did them. He gets on right well with that leg!"

I drank my water and said, "Uh-huh! Yes he do!"

She didn't say nothing as we walked to the door, then she asked me, "What does he do at night with that leg? I mean . . . does he sleep in it?"

I answered, "Chile, if it was you, what would you do?"

She answered, "I blive I'd take it off."

I said, "I blive he do!" And I left.

Two weeks later, they was watching each other pretty good, but they still hadn't said nothing to each other, tho he was working pretty steady over there, early and late. So I went over there with another jug of wine and lied again. He was there putting up some more shelves. Everywhere you could put a shelf, he was putting one! She was letting him!

I sat my mouth and said, "You know, it's a quarintine going on. That virus is taking over! You ain't heard? People got to stay in the house they in, right now, for two days! It's a order! I came to tell you and leave this for medicine." They both stood there looking at me with big round eyes, her stirring spoon in midair and his hammer raised. I went on lying, "I guess you got to stay here a few days, Boxer!" To her I said, "It's a good thing you got that extra room, Oraliza!" I turned to leave before one of them realized I was leaving, so Boxer could too! "Well, I got to rush back cause we quarintined too!" I left.

When I got home I didn't feel bad about nothing! Later, before I went to bed, I bathed, put perfume on and a kinda new nightgown. I'ma have to get some new ones! I rubbed my old husband on his stomach and kissed him all over his face and lips. Turned off the TV and told him, "You are quarintined!"

Now, I didn't hear nothin from Ora nor Boxer in three days, so I went back over there. Boxer was working in the yard. I started to go in the house and he said, "Don't go in there now, she's sleeping." He smiled at me and I went on home. That night when I kissed my husband at the dinner table, he said, "Bertha, what's wrong with you?" I said back, "Ain't that lovin you, babe?" And we laughed.

Next time I saw Oraliza she was bringing my jugs back. She was all smiles, her skin was glowing, her step was light even tho I could see she was tired . . . happy tired.

She said, "I'm bringing your jugs back."

I said, "I see."

"Thank you." She yawned.

"I see." I yawned back.

She smiled a shy smile. "My life is changing."

I smiled. "I see."

She kicked a few pebbles, looking down. "I mean with Boxer."

"I see." I said.

She smiled. "If things keep on being . . . alright . . . you gon mind being my cousin?"

I said, "You all ain't wasting no time."

She said, "Done already wasted enough of that."

"I see."

"Sides, we don't know if we got a lotta time left."

"I see."

She said, "I would stay and talk, but I got to get back."

"I see."

She turned to go, smiling and waving.

I asked her, cause I just happen to think of it, "Ora, what you going to do with that . . . thing you got buried in the chicken house?"

Her eyes got big. "Don't you tell my secret, Bertha!"

I said, "I don't never tell secrets, Ora. I'm known for that!"

She laughed and blushed too. "I'm going to bury it in the field!"

"I see." I thought. "Which field?"

We laughed.

Well, see? I like to have most everything I can in my basement so in case someone needs something . . . or I need something, I will have it! You don't never know what will happen. I like to be prepared, to help me and my friends! I'm known for that!

Spooks*

Now everyone knows that the people of the South are very wise and it is also true that whoever is very wise can be very foolish. However that may be, this is a story of a fine woman by name of Maybelle Brown, a recently widowed woman after thirty years of marriage to Thomas Brown. Now, having married Thomas when she was sixteen years old, the widow Brown was the good ripe age of forty-six years, too young to be alone . . . for long.

Oh, she pined and moaned and mourned for Thomas, she truly did, because she had loved him and been faithful to him in all those years. He had been kind to her and treated her well. Yes . . . Thomas left much to be missed. He was not one of those you are sometimes glad to see go! Having been taken such good care of, the widow Brown was still a good-looking woman . . . a little fat, but in all the places men like a little fat to be sometimes. She was also neat and clean, a good, church-going woman. The preacher never failed to pat her on the back and arms, or knee, if she was sitting, for the fine Christian woman she was. Sister Brown did not fail to appreciate these pats because she missed a man's hand of appreciation since Brother Thomas was gone these past six months.

*Author's note: This story does not pretend to be serious. Written in a moment of relaxation for a little gift of humor.

Other people in the countryside noticed Maybelle also. The women were glad to notice she had settled down to going to church and missing Thomas and not messing with their men! Other men, well, there was one who was a very nice man, Cleveland Jones, lived a mile or so up the road from Maybelle, widowed himself. He was not pleased to see Tom die, but was pleased to see a fine-looking woman like Maybelle alone. He did not want to grow old alone . . . and though there were other single women in the countryside, it was to be considered that Thomas *had* looked satisfied and Maybelle *did* look good and . . . she had a house, too! (Cleveland was not greedy, just sensible.)

Maybelle was a good age, too, not to be making him look like a fool, so Cleveland decided he would work on the future and began to go over to Maybelle's house when she wasn't home and chop plenty of firewood, mow her lawn, fix little things around her house, and smile as he left because he knew how happy she would be and how happy he would be when he let her know how happy he had made her! He enjoyed the little fun of this game and it progressed about five months and the widow still did not know who to be grateful to, but she mightily appreciated it and knew it was a man, which made it even better! Somehow this affected her sexually and she was stirred to think somebody was watching her. Now, she still mourned Thomas, truthfully, but she did it looking better every day.

We all know the Devil is a mighty busy fellow and that he roams the earth and makes many friends. He had a very good close friend that lived down the road from Maybelle on a little rundown piece of land with his wife and children. He went by name of Sam Smith. Now, Sam was always looking for something to do to please the Devil, as I said, he was a good friend to the Devil. The Devil didn't care for Sam much, cause who likes a fool? Sam sure had noticed Maybelle Brown as she passed his house on the way to church or the store and he had taken to walking up the road toward her house, and that's how he come to see Cleveland finishing his work there one day and rushing away. Now, even when the Devil don't like you he will help you cause he likes to see a good show so it didn't take Sam no time to figure out what Cleveland was doing; a few more words with Maybelle and he knew she didn't know who was doing it, or why. As he brought the pieces of the puzzle together, he placed himself right in the middle of it!

"How you like your lawn, Miz Brown?" he asked one day.

"Why, I like it just fine," came the surprised answer.

"I'm glad you are pleased." He smiled broadly.

"Why . . . is it . . . are you—?" She hesitated because she knew he was mostly lazy and he was married, too!

"Now, don't ask no questions you don't need to know the answer to," he volleyed.

And he walked off just as proud and cool as could be, leaving Maybelle Brown looking wonderingly open-mouthed after him before she continued on her way home from the store.

It wasn't too many days before she passed the Smiths' house and saw no one except Mrs. Smith washing clothes in an old tin tub with three or four youngsters playing around her. Sam, who was usually lounging round the gate, wasn't there. Maybelle didn't know Mrs. Smith well so she just waved and passed on by. When she arrived home though, who should she see putting the lawnmower away but Sam! He had timed it right when he saw her coming!

Running toward him she shouted, "Sam Smith! I see you! I see you! So you the one been doing all these nice things for me!" She hit him playfully. "I thought it was you!"

Wiping his brow, Sam answered, "Awwww, Miz Maybelle! I didn't mean for you to catch up with me. I thought I could get away from round here fore you got here . . . cause the yard didn't need much today. I thought I would be gone! Lord a mercy! You done caught up with me!" He hit her playfully on her arm.

"Why you doing all this for me, Sam Smith?"

"Mus I tell you? Don't make me tell you, Miz Maybelle."

"Yes, you tell me! Why? You don't know me that well and you been doing a awful lot of work."

"Yes," he wiped his brow, "it has been a lot, but you alone now and . . . no, I can't tell you all of it."

Bouncing into the house as she spoke, "Let me put my packages in the house and get you some soda, you sweatin and I'll be right back and you tell me why you been doing all these things . . . for me."

Well, Sam closed that door to the toolshed, slamming it, done forgot about that right quick, and strolled over to the back porch. Maybelle hurried out and handed him the glass. "Alright, now, Brother Smith, tell me!"

Sam took the drink, took his handkerchief out and looked serious and even intelligent as he tried to make up his mind to tell her what he had planned to tell her for a month now.

"Well, see, you not going to believe me, cause Brother Brown and I was not close on the outside when people could see, but we was good friends when we had a chance to be."

Maybelle pulled a chair close to Sam. "I didn't know that."

"Yes, we was . . . and Sister, you may not believe this, but many times Brother Brown has spoken with me since he been gone."

"What you sayin', Sam?!"

"That's right!"

"He do? He has?" Excitement and belief in her voice.

"Yes!"

"What does he say?"

"He mostly say things to do for you."

"Ohhh . . . for me." She is pleased so she believed him.

"Yessss . . . he loved you a whole lot." Sam is somber with this task.

"Yes . . . and I loved him." Somberness returned.

"Yes, well, he gone now. We all got to go," Sam prophesied.

"Yes, well, when do he come talk to you?"

"Oh, in the evenings or late at night when he wake me up."

"He wakes you up?"

"Oh yes, he likes it when it is dark, very dark! No lights and no touching."

"And he told you to look after me?" Her voice tender.

"Yes."

"Can I talk to him? Why don't you tell him next time he comes that I want to see him?" She moved closer.

"Can't see him. Wouldn't come back no more! He told me that!" Justa waving his hands.

"Can't see him . . . Well, can I talk to him?"

"I will ask him."

"When?"

"Don't know when . . . have to wait and see."

"See can you call upon him and make him come to you."

"I'll see that tonight!"

"You will?"

"Yes!"

"Ohhhhh, thank you, Brother Smith. Just thank you!" She grabbed him and hugged him . . . like a lady.

"Well, I'm going on now, got things to do." He got up to leave as he handed her the glass.

"Allright . . . and thank you, Sam Smith, for everything."

He just waved his hands in answer.

"You don't have to keep on doing these things. That's an awful lot for me to expect you to do."

"It's alright, it's alright, don't you worry your pretty li'l head about it. It'll be done!" Sam moved away.

"Well, thank you . . . I don't know how to thank you, but, thank you." As I said, she was a good woman.

"'S'alright," Sam threw back into the breeze.

Maybelle had to holler a little now, "Don't forget to ask Thomas for me! I want to talk to him, my husband."

Sam hollered back, "I won't . . . I can't forget."

Maybelle sat back down on the porch looking at the lovely

manicured yard and slowly tapping the glass with her fingers as she thought, "Well, I'll say! I can't hardly believe Thomas, going over there to see Sam Smith. They didn't even hardly talk when he was alive! This yard sure does look fine, though. I'm tellin you, that Sam is a better man than I thought."

With those few words that pleased the Devil she went into her house and shut the door, to lay in bed as she went to sleep and think and think and think.

Needless to say, Sam was there bright and early cause he didn't have much time. No telling when Cleveland would speak up with his piece. Maybelle was already up sitting at the table having tea. She was that kind of lady.

Sam tapped on the screen door. "Maybelle?" Overnight he had dropped "Miz" and "Sister."

"Yes? Oh, Sam Smith." She jumped to the door. "Come in, come in. Have some tea? Did you talk to Thomas? Were you able to get him?"

Sam smiled broadly. "Lord, Maybelle, that man was so glad we finally got together! I told him I didn't know he wanted us to, that's why I was sneakin' and surprising you. But he said no, he wants us to be friends, that you need a friend."

"He did?"

"He did! I could even say he was happy! I couldn't see him, it got to be black dark, you know, but I could tell it in his voice."

"Ohhhhhhh!" Maybelle hollered.

"Now, Maybelle, don't go getting upset now or I won't tell you no more."

"Why can't he come to talk to me?"

"That's the good part."

"It is? What?"

"He said, now listen, he said if I have like a sance or say-ounce, whatever how you say it! If I come here tonight, when it's black dark and sit in the living room, he will try to get through to us. He want you to go into the bedroom and lay down and he said your heart have to be open for him."

"My heart is open for him," Maybelle tendered.

"Nooo, it seem you got to do it a special way."

"A special way?" Now she was no fool, just a good lady.

"Yes, a special way! You got to spread your arms and legs spread-eagle like."

"*Open!*" Maybelle gasped.

"Yes . . . and let me see what else. Oh, yes, you got to be naked."

Maybelle rolled her eyes. "Where you going to be?"

"I'll be in the living room, 'cause he said he want what he say to you to be private."

"Oh . . . alright! Cause if I ain't gon have no clothes on, well, I don't know bout that."

"Now, Maybelle, Sister, your husband wouldn't told me to come over here and do this if I was not a proper person. Now, would he?"

"I guess he wouldn't."

"He was no fool."

"No, he wasn't!"

"So that's settled. Oh yes, you have to leave the door cracked between the living room and the bedroom so his spirit can travel from me to you."

"I thought spirits could go through walls."

"Don't ask me, Sister, just repeating what he said. Say, you better let me take a look at that living room and the bedroom so I can see what he was talkin bout."

"Alright." Maybelle got up to lead the way. "Come on this way." She showed him and he stood, pulling his chin thinking.

"Hem, hemmmmm. Now, I got to come when it's dark, deep in the night, Sister, so you better leave the door cracked. What time you go to bed?"

"I'm going early tonight! It's Saturday anyway, and I got to go to church tomorrow."

"Okay . . . and remember you and me must not talk once he gets here or you will break the spell. You hear?"

"I hear."

"Okay! Brother Brown is mighty excited, I can tell you that!"

"I am too! Go on and go now. I got so many things to do!"

As Sam was leaving, he reminded her, "Now, you ain't gon talk this over with nobody, are you? Cause . . ."

"Oh no!"

"Cause if you do, he might not come. One unbeliever can stop him. You got to help me concentrate, too! Tonight you just concentrate hard as I will."

"Oh, I will, I will."

"And don't spect him to talk too much the first time. He didn't say too much to me the first time."

"Alright."

"Okay. Goodbye now, see you later. No, I won't see you but I will be here."

"Goodbye, Mr. Smith."

"Goodbye."

And he was gone off to enjoy his thoughts of the day, leaving her to enjoy her thoughts of the night.

There is no blackness like the night in the South unless it is the night in the North and this night was no exception. It was *black*! The moon didn't hardly make a dent in it. Maybelle Brown had pulled all the shades down, cracked the door, was in bed early, naked and waiting for it to get blacker. She had bathed and perfumed herself for her husband, he always liked that. She dozed a little and woke up when it was very dark to the sound of Sam Smith entering the back door. She was all crooked in the bed but quickly adjusted herself as she heard Sam whisper, "It's me, Maybelle," and she whispered back, "Okay."

She heard him take a seat and she opened her arms and legs as wide as she could and began to concentrate. I guess they concentrated about ten minutes or so till Maybelle was about to doze off again and she heard a sound. Was it the door? Was it a step? Maybelle held her breath, her heart pounded and her skin became prickly.

"Is that you, Thomas?"

A whispered, "Shhhhhhh, yessssss it's me. I will blow on you to prove I am here, don't move," in a spooky way. Sure enough, she felt a warm breath from her feet to her stomach.

"Ohhhh, it's you," she whispered back.

"*Shhhhhhhhh,* do not talk. The Lord will not let me stay long tonight."

"You got to go already?" Maybelle almost cried.

"Oh my, I've missed you," the ghost whispered and blew on her body again.

"Ohhhhh, I've missed you," she whispered back.

"Oh, my beautiful wife. I can't leave without one more taste of your beautiful body." The spooky whisper was hoarse now.

"Oh Tom, can you do that?"

"Don't talk anymore, I must save my strength. Do not touch me."

"Alright." She was a little afraid so she almost jumped when he touched her, it felt so real, but it soon felt so good she was no longer afraid. She figured he must have learned some things up there or wherever he was, 'cause it felt better than before and he had grown some. She never did hear the bed squeak or feel his weight. Funny about people, but there you are. After an hour or two and many moans and groans, the ghost had to leave and stole away into the living room, into the night.

Maybelle lay there, supine and satisfied as she had not been in so long a time, thinking about Thomas Brown. She had forgotten to ask him to come again! She must ask Sam Smith the first time she saw him again. Lord, she had forgotten him! She raised her head, "Sam?" There was no answer. He must have gone, she thought. She turned over and went into the best sleep she had ever had.

She didn't have to wait long to ask Sam. He was there the next morning.

"Howdy, Maybelle."

"Morning, Sam! Come on in, have some tea. Oh Sam, he was here, he was here!"

"I know it." He smiled. "I felt it! I knew he was coming."

"Well, he sure did!" Maybelle smiled. "We didn't get to talk much tho."

"Told ya you can't talk much to him."

"You do!"

"Well, don't ask me. Them spirited things is strange sometimes."

Maybelle leaned toward Sam. "Well, when is he coming back?"

"Didn't he tell you?"

"*No,* he said don't talk!"

Placing his hand on his chin thinking again, Sam said, "Well, let's see now. When do I mostly get to talk to him? Now, mostly, Wednesday and Saturday. Yeah! Seem like them the days."

"Days?"

"Well, them the nights."

Maybelle looked concerned. "Well, I can't spect you to come over here that late at night two times a week like that!"

Sam looked concerned. "Now, don't you worry your pretty head bout that!"

"You mean, if you have to, if he can't come alone, you will?"

"I sure will! I won't let you down! He is my friend and now you are my friend."

Maybelle looked concerned. "Wonder why he can't come with just me here?"

Sam looked concerned. "It ain't good to wonder too much, Sister, just be thankful, that's all. Well, you have a good day in church, and I'm going home and get me some sleep case he come again tonight and I got to get up and come on over here fore Wednesday."

Maybelle blushed. "You blive he will? Oh, my Lord!"

"You can never tell what a spirit will do, Sister Maybelle. Well, good day, Sister. Say, did you enjoy his visit, Sister?"

"It was a mighty fine visit, Brother, mighty good." Maybelle blushed into the house.

This lasted, these seances, about seven weeks, with Thomas visiting two times, three times, four, even up to seven times a week. Maybelle could not believe her good fortune. Thomas was such a strong lover, not like the once a week it had been before he passed away. Lord, she could hardly wait to die and go wherever he was, heaven or not. But it was most good enough as it was, he came so regular. Sometimes she felt this was better; no washing, no ironing or cooking for nobody but her. All her days belonged to her, do whatever she wanted and yet in the night there was married satisfaction. Lord Jesus! And the Devil smiled.

The only thing wrong was Sam Smith had to always be there. That poor man was so good about everything. Always willing, always willing, God love him. The Devil smiled again. How that Sam could stay up most of the night and still keep up all this work was more than she could understand, and take care of his home life, too! He was a mighty good and a mighty strong man and a good, good friend. Now everybody hearing this tale knows what Sam was thinking cause he went around smiling all the time.

Now Cleveland Jones had long began to notice how much happier Maybelle was looking, but he never saw no man around in the daytime so he didn't know what to think until he thought of looking round at night. Even then he would see all the lights go off as Maybelle went to bed earlier and earlier without no company coming, so he figured it was just cause Maybelle was getting over the passing away of Thomas Brown and he was glad because that meant he could speak up soon. As fate would have it, though, he had to rush away quickly one day when he was stacking the firewood he had cut cause

Maybelle was coming up the road from the sewing circle earlier than usual. He snatched his shirt off a nail and trotted off through the woods to his own house. He was home fore he missed his watch he had hung on a nail and knew he had to go back to get it or his plan would not be the kind of surprise he had planned for Maybelle.

So, after dark he went and had his watch and was smiling at the goodness of Maybelle being in bed asleep already when he saw someone coming stealthily up to the house. He stepped back into the shadows and watched as Sam Smith stepped softly up the steps and pushed on the door and it *opened*! Not only that, Sam went on in! And two hours later he hadn't come *out*! And when he did come out he was tucking his shirt in his pants and he was *smiling*!! Wellllllll . . . "That ole bitch!" a brokenhearted Cleveland said as he kicked a few trees on his way home.

Needless to say, the lawn grew over, the wood got used and none was replaced. Things started breaking down outside and nobody fixed them. Sam noticed before Maybelle did, but she finally did, too.

"Sam, you must be tired all these nights you come over here to help me and Thomas."

Sam looked around the yard. "Yeah, my back been gettin at me a little bit more lately. Just look at this yard! I got to get to it."

"Well, I sure do appreciate it," smiled Maybelle.

Sam looked at Maybelle sideways. "Guess maybe Thomas would understand if I didn't sit here to bring him a week or so, so's I can go on and get this wood chopped and this grass out."

Maybelle jerked out her answer, "Oh no! No, no, no! I got to see Thomas every time I can! No! No! You don't have to do it! I'll find someone else to do this yard. This ain't nothing to worry 'bout. No, no, you just keep coming when you can so I can be with Thomas as much as I can!"

"Well, alright, if you say so. Then pretty soon I'll be able to take up the chores again."

I'm sure you didn't guess that the person Maybelle asked to take over her yard and cut wood was Cleveland Jones. Well, it was! And Cleveland Jones, a little sneaky, said, "Why don't you ask Sam Smith? Can't he do it?"

"Well no, you see his back done gone bad on him."

"Maybe he use it too much!"

"Well, I don't know, but he use to do it and now he can't no more."

"He used to do it?!" Cleveland frowned.

"Oh yes! I didn't know it for a long time, then one day I caught him putting the tools away and found out it was him all the time!"

Now Cleveland started thinking right quick and said, "Well, is that so? Wasn't that nice of him? Doing all that work? For nothing, too!"

Maybelle was serious. "Well, it seems like Thomas and he were friends and I didn't know nothing about it."

"How long was you married to Tom, Maybelle?"

"Thirty years."

As Maybelle continued talking, Cleveland looked at her a little harder, thinking. "There's more fool in some of us than a quick look will tell," but he wasn't so mad at her as he was before, so he listened.

Maybelle lowered her voice. "You know what, Brother Cleveland?"

"No, what, Sister Maybelle?"

"Thomas comes to me through Sam Smith!"

"What you mean, 'comes' to you?"

"I mean Sam and he were such good friends that Thomas comes to see me if Sam is there!"

Cleveland leaned forward. "In the dark?"

"Oh, yes, it's got to be in the dark! Can't come in no light!"

Cleveland leaned closer. "What does Tom talk about? What does he say?"

Well, Maybelle just blushed so much that she didn't even

have to tell Cleveland Jones nothing 'cause he could see it right there on her face . . . pleasure.

Maybelle rolled her eyes and said, "It's private, just between a man and his wife!"

"You know, Sister Maybelle, Tom is gone now and you oughta start thinking of a new life. I'm sure Tom would want you to be happy."

"Ohhh, I *am* happy!" she assured him.

"I mean all day as well as all night," he replied.

"Oh, as long as I have Thomas, I will be happy. But Brother Cleveland, please don't tell another soul! Sam says if an unbeliever knows, Thomas will stop coming."

"Yes, I can see what Sam means," Cleveland said very seriously. "He sure has been a going between."

"Well, what about my yard, Brother Cleveland? You can see Brother Sam can't do it if his back is hurting, and besides, Thomas comes so often, Sam don't get much sleep sometimes . . . and I preciate what he do to bring Tom to me so I am asking you this."

Now Cleveland is thinking clearly and his understanding is good. He thinks Maybelle is a bigger fool than he might want for his wife, but, after all, she is a woman, a good woman, and that Sam is smart, so he said, "All right, I'll take care of the yard and fix things round your house, outside . . . and inside!"

"What will you charge me?" Maybelle smiled up at him.

"Nothing, just dinner every Sunday."

"Why, that's fine . . . Early, after church."

"Don't matter what time, I'm going to spend the evening with you."

"Oh Cleveland, Thomas wouldn't like . . ."

"Thomas, God rest his soul, is dead, Maybelle."

"Yes, but he . . ."

"I'm not going to try to take nothing from you or Thomas, ain't trying to sleep with you, just gonna talk."

"Well then, you welcome."

"See you Sunday then, Maybelle."

That Sunday Cleveland looked that house over good and found him a place to hide where he could see everything he wanted to. I think the bathroom opened into a closet and the bedroom so that was his way, and one night he didn't go home after working till it was dark. He just waited till her lights were out then creeped back into the house. He didn't have to be too lucky cause Sam came pretty regular and so he watched Sam go through his act. It liked to broke his head cause he was so mad at Sam, and his heart cause he really wanted Maybelle for his wife, but after Sam was gone he heard Maybelle call out, "Sam, he gone now, you can go." So he knew she was a foolish woman and he called out to her in a whisper, spookier than Sam's:

"*Sammmmmmmmmm* issss gooonnnnnee. Weeeee dooooon't *neeeeed* him noooooooooooooo mooooooooooooooore!"

"Oh Thomas, I am so glad, you mean there is just me and you from now on?"

"Yesssss, just *meeeeee* and *youuuuuuu*! Noooooo mooooo Sam! IIIII doooooon't like him noooooo mooooooore! I want you to marry up with Cleveland, I b'lieve."

See, he realized he may not want to marry her without first trying it to see. Sam might be a fool, too! So he said, "I want to hold you once more before I depart this world forever."

"Thomas, you mean you not coming here no more?" Alarmed.

"Noooooo, and I don't want Sam to eitheeeerrrrrr!"

"Not even to clean the yard when his back gets better?"

"To do noooooothing, no more, neverrrrrrrrr. You get Cleveland. Now get ready, I am coming to you again."

See, Cleveland had been getting undressed all the time in the dark and so he made love to Maybelle, who was holding up awful well, though she kept saying to him, "You too much, Thomas. Lord a mercy, you something!"

Cleveland sneaked out too after saying, "Now, remember, Cleveland Jones is your future husband."

"Alright, Thomas, but spose he don't want me?"

"Work on him. You will know what to do! I want you to be happy."

"Alright, Thomas."

"Goodbye."

He stole away.

Now Maybelle slept heavy, heavy, heavy that night and she was awakened by Sam at the door demanding his coffee and breakfast as had become his habit lately. She grabbed a robe and rushed to the door, opened it but left the screen hooked.

"You can't come here no more, Sam!"

"What you mean? What's wrong with you, woman?"

"Thomas told me!"

"Thomas told you what? Are you crazy!"

"Told me you can't come here no more!"

"When he told you that?"

"Last night after you left! He stayed to . . . talk awhile."

Sam's eyes grew big and deep in thought as he asked, "Last night . . . he stayed?"

"Yes, and I don't know what you did, but he don't like you no more so don't come back! It ain't my fault. I'm sorry but I got to do like he says . . . you said that yourself!"

"Yes, I said that."

"Well, goodbye then."

"Who gon' look out for you?" Sam bent over, peeping through the crack she left open.

"Cleveland Jones. Thomas wants that."

"Tom wants that, huh?"

"That's what he said, so goodbye."

"When is Tom coming again?" Sam was persistent.

"He said maybe never." Maybelle was exasperated.

"Never?! That's a long time!"

"Death is a long time, that's what you said." With those words she closed the door.

So to make a long story short, Cleveland and Maybelle were married as soon as the year was out and her mourning for Thomas was over. Of course, some of those evenings Cleveland stayed too late after supper on a Sunday and had to sleep on the couch in the living room, Thomas came by to see Maybelle and tell her how wise she was to choose Cleveland Jones and to make love to her for the last time. Sam Smith never came again, but for a long, long time, anytime he and Cleveland happened to pass on the street or at the store, they took a good long look at each other and kept right on passing on by.